Cover Art by Kavita Kharecha

ISBN-13: 978-1-7332332-9-3

Distributed by Ingram

Galaxy Galloper Press, LLC
2 Tearose Lane
Levittown, PA 19054
galaxygalloper@gmail.com

Dedication:

to the doc sabhs

Where the Sun Will Rise Tomorrow

RASHI ROHATGI

Chapter One

"They say the sun rises in Japan earlier than anywhere else," I tell my sister. We are waiting for it ourselves from a small rowboat in the middle of the cool, fresh Ganges River, and I trail my fingers in the water as I look east. The sky has taken on a burnt orange tinge, and from experience we know we have about ten minutes until it is blazing above us and we must head back to return our craft to the temple boathouse on the riverbank.

Maya flicks her wrist and sprays me, enough to tease, not to drench. Now that we all have to wear these widow's weeds, we can't go around getting soaked through like the heroines in the romances we hide under our pillows. "They say? Has Nash enlisted all of his friends to write to you now, too?" She mock-pouts. "If so, I should think I deserve to read at least a few of them."

"I read it in our geography textbook," I insist, even though she is right. My fiancé, Nash, has been in Tokyo for the past three excruciating years on an engineering scholarship, writing me a weekly letter without fail—and without any mention, thankfully, of engineering. Though he could have finished up by August, I imagine he's relieved that the British have recalled all of the Indian students from Japan. He's only ever wanted to be a historian, and without a qualification it may be easier for him to avoid joining Prithviraj and Sons, Chandrapur's foremost bridge designers and train track planners.

Maya can generally see through my lies, but the mention of textbooks lights her up just as brightly as the quickly-appearing sun. "God, I've been going back through them, too. Can you believe how lucky we are? Two more years of fun."

"Two more years of school," I amend, although if she wants, after, she'll be able to teach her own class in Kansara and be in school forever. I remind her as much. Now that Nash is coming home, I'm not so keen to spend two years training to be a teacher— that's one qualification I'm sure I'll never use—but more than that, I'm relieved that my marriage and Maya's won't be happening simultaneously. I love

Nash, and I love his family compound, with its elegant lemon-yellow columns and filigree windows, but the thought of leaving my sister tightens my chest and slows my breath. Still, it is only two streets away. And still, I am older, if only by a year; I need to impress upon her that these two years will still be followed by the rest of her life—one she must come to terms with, and hopefully, learn to enjoy.

She cocks her head, giving it decent consideration. I begin to row us back to shore, slowly, the heat of the metal oar handle growing warmer every second under my palms. "It's an option," she says, finally, taking up her own oar. "Although who knows what could happen in two years? Who I could meet?"

"Hush," I say, but she carries on.

"Even our very own Asoka married for love—twice. And he didn't make those girls stay in some backwater village."

It's not fair of her to use my slight Asoka obsession against me. Slight, I maintain, and justified: under him, our town was the centre of the world. Today, the girls in our class—the girls formerly in our class, I should say, now that we've all graduated from Bankipore Girls High School—take every opportunity to tell us how much better Calcutta is,

9

how much worldlier, how much more important. "The other three times he married out of duty," I remind her, but lightly. We've reached the shore, and the young priest is tying up the boat. We nod to him, and to the Shiva lingam in his temple, so that our early morning 'prayer expedition' is not quite a lie. We straddle the line between propriety and waywardness as it is, coming out alone—but we have one another, and everyone knows our father indulges us in everything, including freedom.

"It's a new world," Maya says, hopping up into the carriage that has been waiting for us and extending me a helping hand. I take it and join her in the relieving shade. "They have films now, and automobiles. Two years ago we never would have dreamt that we'd get a teacher training college. Two years from now the whole world may be unrecognizable. Why not dream up a place for ourselves within it?"

I am happy with my place in the world I have—but I, too, want nothing more than for Maya to stay beside me. Her fiancé's family seems like a good bunch, but as they are more closely related to my mother—dead in the '99 plague before Maya's films and automobiles—we haven't seen much of them. Maya will have to deal with the unknown, all right, while I will get to deal with Nash, who is so close to home, so close to being mine that I can taste it. I take her hand in mine and squeeze. "To the future."

We sit down to breakfast with Papa when we get home; though we've gotten used to seeing each other in drab white, he still winces at the sight of us. "All of those silks, just wasting away in the cupboard," he says, tucking into his paratha and yogurt.

I eat as well, clarified butter dripping down my fingers—our cook has been with us for ages, and since we heard the news of Nash's impending return she has been spoiling me. Maya steals a bite off my paratha and says, "I have an idea, though," as if she doesn't have a perfectly good breakfast sitting in front of her.

"Oh?" Papa never notices.

"Leela and I should take a look at everything and get her trousseau organized," she says. "Otherwise how are we going to know what we'll need to buy as soon as the boycott ends? It could end just three days before the wedding and then we'd be stuck."

"It may not end even then," he says, "but that's still a good idea. You'll have all summer to make any of the things you lack: lace or whatnot."

We stare at him. Of course, he continues eating.

"Papa," I say, "you don't think either of us knows how to make lace, do you? You sent the ayah away when I was twelve!"

"You said you didn't need her any longer," he argues. "By the time my sister was twelve, she could make lace, and embroider, and manage a whole house. She would have had to, too—she was married at fourteen."

We are getting quite long in the tooth, we know, at fifteen and sixteen, and Koyal Chachi, our aunt and Papa's sister-in-law, has certainly not kept her mouth shut about the gaps in our education. This is what comes of a father letting his girls run the house, she's said time and again, and in general, I think things have worked out marvelously. But now I realize that living British-style, with no family or guidance, I have no idea what belongs in a trousseau, and absolutely no idea how to make any of the things I lack—and, during this boycott, no idea where to buy them. I'm proud of our locally-made goods, but why couldn't Banarasi silk have become the symbol of that pride?

Maya catches my eye. "Cotton lingerie," she whispers.

We giggle, but she must be apprehensive, too, because when Papa sends his empty plate to the kitchen, she drags me up to Mumma's closet without missing a beat.

We don't open the closet immediately. Instead, we stand in front of it, and I am sure Maya is remembering the same day I am. Neither of us avoids Papa's room: it gets the best light in the house early in the evenings, after school but before he returns from the office, so we generally flop ourselves on his bed and read until the sun dies down. His own closet is full of identical cotton pyjama sets and coffee-colored woolen suits, well made but boring. It sits next to his desk, a grand wooden affair with twenty-seven small drawers. In the third one from the bottom, second row from the left is his key ring, and on it is the tiny silver key to my mother's possessions.

It was the last day of the year, and the last day of the century, and the skies above our house were bright with fireworks. Papa had gone to the Sinha's annual party: at that age, we'd almost still believed that it was just a chore, a duty to be gotten through before he'd come home and celebrate with us over ice creams. Almost, except we'd been poking our heads out of his bedroom window, overlooking the busy street—our little, modern house, on the edge of the City's compounds—instead of gorging ourselves on toffee. We'd seen him leave, not with his briefcase but instead with an open bottle of champagne in one hand and two flutes in the other, and greet an open carriage. Somehow, at the moment, I'd still thought he'd run into her by chance, but Maya had grabbed my hand at that point, and I knew that the Anglo-Indian woman in the black sari—I recognized her from Holi and Diwali celebrations, but I was certain we'd never been introduced—had not been casually driving by.

I'd pulled Maya away from the window and marched her to the desk. "Tonight," I told her, "we're going to have a look at what is ours."

We'd never told Papa about our first perusal of Mumma's closet, not that night and not a few years later when, upon the ayah's departure, we'd insisted that we were ready to wear her saris instead of frocks and been overruled by Chachi and her practical suggestion that our school uniforms were quite enough for the moment. We'd been careful not to move anything, so careful we barely took anything in beyond the panoply of colors, the rustle of fabrics, the faint smell of jasmine and musk.

This time, Maya opens the closet door, and her voice is steady as she says, "I'll need half of this, so choose what you like, but be fair."

"As if I'm ever not," I say, taking a sari of midnight blue silk between my fingers. There is nothing white in this closet; even the drabbest cotton petticoat is a pale peach. I sit, and pull out a pair of sandals. "Will these fit us, do you think?"

Maya kneels beside me, a golden blouse in her lap that would be perfect for my wedding if I can convince her I need it. "When we were twelve, maybe," she says.

I shake my head. "I think I can manage." My feet are almost as long as hers, but they are narrower, somehow—nothing like Papa's, so I must have gotten them from Mumma. I slide it on, and feel what I'd been missing at graduation, what with our places at the training college settled: a sense of adulthood. I begin to smile until I hear tiny heaving sounds coming from my now curled-up sister. "It's okay," I tell her.

"It's not," she mumbles, and of course, she's right. She should have tried the shoes on years ago.

I don't say anything about the blouse, but that night, I dream of my wedding day. I lead Nash around the fire, my breasts golden, my sari blood red, my stride purposeful.

Maya and Papa are reading in the living room, but I cannot concentrate. Nash is meant to get back any day now; two other Japan-returnees, Sapan Jha and Yogesh Agarwal, have already come. It's just a matter of ships and trains. Each day I try to keep my cool until 4pm, the scheduled arrival time for the Calcutta-Banaras line, but the evenings are a waste. I can't study, like Maya does: she studied every second of every day in order to be allowed to start school with me, afraid even as a new motherless child of five of being left behind, and sometimes it feels as though she has never stopped studying. Instead, I fritter my time away making shaky rangolis in the courtyard and lining the drive with tea lamps that blow out each night. I stare at myself in the mirror and practice making faces that convey passion and desire.

"Let's go to the djinni mosque," Maya says. It's a good suggestion; its spirit-filled grounds are even spookier at night, and, they say, luckier. But it's far—we would have to take a carriage—and I don't want to be out of earshot when Nash's parents come to let me know he's back. I shake my head.

"Let's go ask Sonuji to teach us how to make fruitcake," she offers; our cook is cousin sisters with the cook at the Bankipore Club and gets all the latest British recipes. She wants to serve fruitcake at the mehndi ceremony, which Papa has agreed to, but I am not sure.

"There's a sugar boycott on, darling," Papa reminds her. Until Bengal is un-partitioned—until we get a larger say in our own governance—we've promised not to have anything nice.

I sigh, but I didn't want to get my hands covered in oil, either—just in case.

"Let's go on the terrace," she says, finally, and I shrug, and she gets up.

It's glorious up here, the day's heat retreating and a balmy breeze lapping at our toes. I can't see it from here, but I face the train station anyways. "What were you reading about?" I ask.

She answers, but I stop listening. A bicycle rickshaw has stopped at our gate, and the night watchman has started opening the gate without calling up to Papa to confirm—but only one person I know would travel to our home in a bicycle rickshaw lugging a case behind him.

I fly down the stairs, ignoring the fact that I haven't pinched my cheeks red in the past hour, or oiled my hair in several days, or snuck on kajal or lipstick. I don't even hate my ghostly attire: it means that I light up the night, and Nash sees me running towards him as soon as I reach the drive.

We shouldn't be hugging like this. We should never have considered touching, and in fact before we left, though Maya was a fair and unobtrusive chaperone on our trips to all of Chandrapur's historical sites, we'd never have dared to hold hands, especially out in the open. But here, under the same sky after so long, his hands around my waist feel right. My hands around his neck—he's grown somehow leaner and more firm than I'd remembered — feel like they've found their haven. Nash's head is buried in my neck, and I smell the seawater on his hair.

"Nash! You haven't even gone home yet!"

He pulls his face up, and simultaneously pulls me closer to him. Staring into his doe-lashed eyes, feeling his rough cotton tunic on my midriff, I am intoxicated. "I had to see you, Leela." His voice is gruff, and I stare at his lips. I want to bridge the final gap between us, and bring his face to mine. The shadows cast by the tea lights fall on both our cheeks — we glitter like stars.

"I've waited for you," I whisper to him, instead, and he smiles. I close my eyes, soaking in this moment.

"Avinash, beta," says my father, and I jump out of Nash's arms so fast I almost step into a lit lamp. Maya steps forward from behind Papa and adjusts my pleats so I am less likely to burst into flame. "Very good to see you, though of course not best pleased you are back."

"Papa!" Maya admonishes.

Nash is still smiling, however. "Agreed, Uncleji, on both accounts, but we must take it as a good sign: the Brits are scared. They know, now, that we can best them."

I attempt to shoo my father away with dirty looks, the way I do to lizards upon entering an empty room. As usual, I am unsuccessful. Nash is speaking with his hands now, about the war and the political mood in Calcutta and the boycott, and there are no more traces, now, on his body, of the moment we shared. I find it harder to steady my own skin.

"Come, have tea," says Papa, finally, after I have watched my family usurp my betrothed after an extremely lengthy absence; even Maya was contributing, filling in Nash on the mood in town. If Curzon would just reverse his decision—show any sign of taking heed of his Indian subjects—most of us would be satisfied, but there are always editorialists pushing to take the boycott further, calling for open rebellion until Independence. Unrest, but at least the partition of Bengal has given the Hindus of Chandrapur the centrality we had so many eons ago.

"I'll make it," I offer, though I am terrible at it—I can never get the skin of the milk to do what I want—and will be calling upon Sonuji to help me.

He shakes his head at all of us, but smiles at me. "Not tonight," he says. "I'm sure the news of my arrival has reached my parents by now, and they are presumably impatient."

"It was very improper of you to stop here," says Maya, "but then, you probably couldn't resist, could you?" I stop myself from elbowing her because I quite like the blush that rises on Nash's cheeks.

"We'll come and visit you at home tomorrow," I tell him.

"Rest up and get ready for a new day," says Papa.

Nash nods his goodbyes, and Papa and Maya turn to leave as the gate closes. From the back of the rickshaw, Nash blows me a kiss, and I catch it in my palm.

The next day my cheeks, my eyes, and my hair are as good as they're going to be when Nash arrives just after breakfast. Instead of inviting us to his family's for lunch, he is taking Maya and me to Gol Ghar. Everybody, from children to grandparents,

21

loves Gol Ghar, but I wonder if he's chosen the grain silo so that we will have an excuse to walk hip to hip, shoulder to shoulder up the narrow staircase. As Maya tells him about the good luck we've had with the training college's opening, I study him.

Nash has always been beautiful: his dark skin smooth, his broad lips projecting softness, his lashes longer than mine with three coats of petroleum jelly. Beautiful, and somehow therefore gentle: the Chowdhurys have always been successful, and lucky, and generous. They have nothing to prove, and Nash, a diamond in this fine setting, even less so. And so though he's always been tall, and always looked at each person as though they were the only one left in the city, he's always struck me as laughing, comforting, with kindness to spare. In childhood, we hardly saw anything of him, but once we were formally engaged, he withstood the taunts of his classmates and often swung by with ices or samosas or the choruses of songs from the latest films. It was easy for him to love, and as all I'd ever dreamed of was loving someone back, he was perfect.

He's changed: his lanky frame has tightened, straightened, and as he listens to Maya, I can see in the stiffness of his hands in his lap and of his toes, curled around the edge of his sandals, that he's kept the tiniest portion of his attention for himself. He is still beautiful, but also... threatening? Is that the right word for the way he makes my body, still seated and composed, feel called to attention against any inclination of its own? His hair is longer, I see—his barber must only have shaved him this morning, rather than give him the accompanying trim—and this imperfection lets me catch my breath.

The carriage is pulling up to the Gol Ghar—our very own Round House, our silly English silo that once held grain and now serves as a pleasure ground for those of us too brown to make use of the club—as Nash responds to Maya's exclamation that she's more than ready for us to go back to school next week. "But surely..." he says.

When Nargis and Mawiyya do that to me in school—trail off in the middle of a thought there's no chance I could finish on my own—it's to mock me, but Nash doesn't mock. I realize that while Maya and I have had numerous conversations about my post-marriage life and how to keep it as seamless a transition as possible, Nash and I haven't had any. "Why don't you run slightly ahead and check on the crowd?" I ask Maya with our shared look. We trail her, slowly, and I want to throw my arms around him again, but instead I say, "You know I won't attend the training college from August if you or your parents don't approve." I start with what Maya would call a barefaced lie because I suppose that, all said and done, it's the truth. November, really, is wedding season, but ours is to be held as soon as the weather settles. Some families need time to negotiate; ours will be efficiently put together as Papa has ceded complete control to the Chowdhurys since, as even Koyal Chachi would agree, there's no chance of their taste being anything less than impeccable.

"Oh, no, of course I wouldn't dream of stopping you!" he says. He actually stops, and turns to me, and reaches for my hands before he realizes, and stops himself. "Leela, I didn't realize you wanted to become a teacher, but I should have guessed. You've read all of the great histories of Chandrapur, and your Sanskrit is far better than mine. I've no right or desire to stop you making the most of yourself."

"Well, that's good, then," I say. "Though if I'm being honest, I mostly just want to attend the school to make sure I'm able to see Maya every day. I'm not used to a joint household and I'm not sure I'll be able to play a dutiful daughter-in-law without her as a sounding board." I pause, but Nash smiles, and laughs. "And after suffering through a mixed education, I think it will be nice to have the chance to teach in the Hindu school whenever it opens."

We have only taken a few steps, but already Nash stops, causing the mother and daughter behind us to bump into our calves and mumble apologies. "Leela," he murmurs, so softly I have to lean in to hear, and the proximity is causing my heart to do a furious dance. But then he keeps walking.

"Leela," he says again after a few steps. "When I was in Japan, at first it was terribly lonely. We tried to integrate, but without eating fish, we Hindu students found ourselves isolated in the canteen; without much money, additionally, I found myself unwilling to hole up and play cards with boys from

Lucknow or Kanpur. I know you didn't have it easy at Bankipore, either, with your father in trade."

I nod.

"But after the triumph against the West, it was as though divisions had melted away. Even when we were sent home, I knew I was coming back to something important, and the sight of you in that swadeshi sari running towards me solidified every commitment I'd hardly understood, before Tokyo, that I'd had. I've dreamt about you in red for years," he says, and though I want to faint I press my hands to the wall and keep myself barely upright, "but for the past year, I've dreamt about you in white. I'm so lucky that my life partner shares my dreams, not only for us, but for the country." Nash sees me faltering, and risks censure from the auntie behind us by steadying me, a hand to the small of my back. I am dizzy for so many reasons.

"I just cannot understand why there is no hesitation towards a communal training college that will only lead towards a communalization of the school system itself, when we're fighting, desperately, against communalism!"

We have almost climbed to the top; I see Maya awaiting us, and when she catches my eye, she winks, but I can't reciprocate. "It wasn't a British initiative," I tell him. "The Director of Schools wanted to keep us girls together, in fact, and then both the Nawab and the Maharani joined together to oppose him. There are surely more than twelve Hindu girls in Chandrapur who may have wanted to get educated alongside us, and soon there will be places, and teachers for them. Education can only help us."

I am out of breath, but we've climbed Gol Ghar, and the view is rewarding enough to let me tear my eyes away from Nash for a minute. And thank heavens, because looking at this new Nash while he is deliberating is… no, not threatening. Unsettling, I decide on. I wink at Maya, and we play our usual game of identifying all of the best places: the fields, in the distance, past the river, where on the way to Gaya we always stop, much too soon, for the best roasted corn; the Rama temple with the most rambunctious monkeys; the Sikh gurudwara that is unquestionably our most beautiful building; the Khudabaksh library where the real scholars spend their days with microscopes, studying the beautifully illuminated manuscripts; the market, where one day soon we must go and see what Indian-made lingerie I will wear to start my married life.

Nash speaks up again, finally. "I've missed this place so much."

There are the beginnings of tears at the corners of his eyes, and I don't know what to say.

Maya never has this problem. "And didn't you miss us, then? I didn't get even one letter from you, Mister."

She has cracked the gloomy spell, and Nash rifles through his bag until he hits upon a small wrapped package. "I thought you'd prefer the paper," he says, handing it to her.

"You didn't have to get her a gift," I say, knowing what it has cost his family to send him away, and all for a trip with no degree certificate.

"But he did," Maya says, as though he'd take it back, ripping it open willy-nilly instead of properly, neatly. I lean over to get a better look, and am glad I did: he's brought her stationary more beautiful than I have ever seen. The British have their formal, heavy paper to announce their galas, and I've coveted that often enough, but this is its opposite: thin, almost translucent, and sparkling, oyster pink with sea-green filigree adorning its edges. Maya is staring at it, and I squeeze her shoulders. "Oh, yes," she says. "Thank you."

She walks ahead of us on the way down, staring at it; it is a good thing, after all, that we've been here countless times before. Nash and I pretend to watch her, to stop her from falling off the edge, but really we are stealing glances at one another. "Thank you," I tell him, and just for a moment, before our feet reach the solid ground, he takes my hand.

Chapter Two

"Bunmai kaika," Nash says, nibbling away at a wheat savory out of the bowl Maya and I have brought over. He's either so entranced by my beauty or engrossed in what he's saying—surely no one can find the Japanese that interesting?—that he's managed to ignore their oily sogginess. I couldn't get the dough tough enough before frying, but we had no excuse for coming over empty-handed. "It means 'civilization and enlightenment,' and they would find our racial and caste prejudices so horribly old-fashioned: they've managed to adapt to Western technology just fine, no kow-towing to Westerners required."

We nod. Asoka'd been calling for an end to prejudices ages ago; in the villages, perhaps, the lower castes and Muslims still found themselves ostracized, but I hardly thought it was still the case here. And as the boycott spread, we were showing ourselves to be just as cosmopolitan, just as capable of speaking our minds, as anyone else in the Empire. "But what about Edward?" I have to ask.

Now Nash does stop his nibbling. "What about Edward?"

I want to pause and soak in Nash's gaze, and when I do so, just for a second, I can imagine, from the tilt of his head, the crinkling of the skin around his eyes, that he is doing the same. "Well…" I wave my hand to mean: 'well, everything about Edward.' The emperor is so chic. No matter how many electric lights they install throughout Tokyo, their emperor will never be as chic as ours.

"And then those cane farmers," Maya agrees, and I know she is looking at Nash and me and thinking of Kansara. The three of us can loll about in Nash's family's front room for as long as it takes Nash to eat the bowl of mattri, but in the village, things will be different. For rural wives, even prosperous ones, relaxation and mixed company are concepts as foreign as Tolstoy's anarchy. "Surely to say we're all the same is to diminish the very power of education that gives us the opportunity to discuss it?"

31

"Rural teachers are the very vanguard of the revolution," I affirm. Just because the very thought of meeting someone half as dashing as Edward — half as dashing as Nash! — in a village is as strange as the thought of Edward on the moon, well — we all have sisters. Though Nash doesn't, actually, for better or worse. They all went, of the same plague year that took Mumma, before anyone outside of the house had a chance to get to know them. I smile at him to encourage him to encourage Maya.

He doesn't say anything, but he does, popping another savory in his mouth, look from me to Maya and back again. Then he stands up. "That's exactly right!"

Hmm, perhaps I need to trust that he needs no encouragement, and that encouragement is in fact overkill. I feel I should stand up, too, but I have sat in exactly such a pose as hides the rolls of my stomach under the pallu of my sari, and if we're not actually leaving, it's best to appear too languid to move. But then a lizard, unsettled by Nash's leap to his feet, falls from the ceiling onto the edge of my toes, and I leap up anyway. I am in a state of total disarray, while Nash is still holding the bowl in one hand like the most elegant waiter in a film set in Berlin, but it doesn't matter. We are standing face to face, and we are both suffused with warmth. Though somehow I wonder if there is something I'd forgotten about him during his time in Japan, something brighter than warmth, something surprisingly dazzling, or dazzlingly surprising. Either way: I'm not entirely sure what is going to happen next, which means I'm not entirely happy.

"Leela," he says, clasping my wrist—though he should not be clasping my wrist, it seems Maya has decided that there is something of a grey area about whether she has to clear her throat, as it's not exactly like holding hands—"I'd not even thought of it like that, but you're right, of course. Whilst I'm relegated to tearoom discussions about meetings and marches, you both are right in the middle of things. Let the teachers themselves teach the politicians what they're ignoring!"

"Indeed," says Maya, airily, from her corner, where she has tucked her feet underneath her and is fidgeting with the end of her plait, "but what exactly do you mean?"

33

"What better way to convince the Nawab and the Maharani to re-integrate schools than by direct action from the trainee teachers themselves? You can prepare a petition, and then deliver it as a group, reminding them that communalism only fuels Edward's stronghold. And then if the entire educated populace of West Bengal demands liberty…" His fingers tighten on my wrist, but his eyes are looking through me to the city, the country, the world he saw in Japan that I will never see, nor wish to.

I must bring my Nash back, even if it means slipping my wrist from his fingers. "Nash, we cannot do that."

He is looking at his empty fingers, and Maya must see how close I am to giving myself back, for she repeats my statement and continues, "Nor would we want to. You may have been too busy in Japan to notice, but we're not exactly friends with those girls."

I cringe. How could Nash, who is friends with everybody, understand? Perhaps he will assume that the fault lies with us. In that perhaps he is correct—partially. The fault lies with me. If we had just been cultureless merchant's daughters, or perhaps just that and motherless, it might have ended with pity. Why had I been so insufficiently accustomed to pity? I taught Maya to have pride, to be sour, to answer back.

Nash's eyes move from his fingers to me. His face is even. "You could be."

"It's too late," I remind him.

"No one could fault you for having tea with your old schoolmates," he says. "It's what I do all day, on the face of it, while studying." When we start college, it has been decided that Nash will finish his engineering certificate via correspondence. I should talk to Nash more explicitly about alternatives to Prithviraj, but I don't want Maya to overhear me utter the word 'alternative.'

Maya scoffs. "People can find fault with us for anything, especially social teas with Muslims. Your parents, for example, would worry about Leela, then, wouldn't they?" Then she stands up, too. "That being said, and discretion assumed, I think we should do it."

What? I say to her with my eyes. Yes: I am here, in the house of my betrothed, not two feet from him, and my eyes are on my sister, the newly-minted revolutionary. "Please come back to earth, Maya. And you, too, Nash."

"Leela—"

"It's time for us to go," Maya says, reaching over, plucking the savories bowl out of his hand. "If we're going to do this, we'll need to get better at this mattri malarkey."

We have ushered Sonuji out of the kitchen with promises to remember to make fork holes in the dough. It seems a foreign room all its own, or maybe the disarray I'm feeling has spread to my relationship with my own house. Maya and I have hardly spent time in the kitchen, it's true: we thought books were more important, yes, but also… Sonuji kept to herself, now, but ten years ago, when my mother was newly gone, she'd been loquacious in her grief. I'd started asking ayah to fetch the snacks so that I didn't have to hear a story about Mumma's deft hand with the khaja. Now, I rummage through the cupboard for the honey—just to snack on while we cook, it's not part of the ingredient list—and find it's not where I'd seen it last.

"I don't think Koyal Chachi will be okay with our making trips to the Khajekalan mohalla just like that; we'll have to tell her we're interested in the Islamic art in the mosque. That way if any word gets through to the Chowdhurys, it can all be spun as cultural interest. And it is interesting, so that's okay. Do you know anything about it, though?"

"Maya," I finally tell her, now that we are alone, and it's quiet, "I don't want to do this. I'm glad to be free of Mawiyya and her retinue. I want to keep going to college without them. Don't you?"

She doesn't turn to face me; she's looking out the window at the courtyard where our clothes are hung out to dry, and she shrugs. "I hate them, but I love you more."

I study the curve of her back. She is standing up uncharacteristically straight. Some new feeling of turmoil begins to curdle in my stomach. "It's okay, Maya. Nash won't throw me over if we don't do it."

She turns her neck to look at me. She's not an owl, so she doesn't quite make it. "He might. He's grown different in Japan."

"He's back," I whisper. "He's back to marry me."

"He's back because he was called back," she says. She turns her neck back to the courtyard, where a wide blue sky is visible. We are in those perfect weeks before the monsoons where one can go anywhere. Even to places heretofore unconsidered.

Maya and I are sitting amongst the aloe blooms in Nash's family compound, starched lilies amongst the delicate tendrils. Sonuji's milkcake has already been taken out and passed amongst Nash's father's younger brother's wives—the youngest, Seema Chachi, is pouring the tea. His mother invited us to be present for the tailor's visit, and she hovers around Nash inspecting the quality of the thick black suit he is wearing. He stands on a wicker stool like a Roman statue, smiling patiently, not sweating at all. When his mother tuts, he smiles at her, at his aunts, at all of us.

"You've grown skinny," his mother says. "Masterji will have to take it in as well as embroider."

"I daresay he can do it, Amma," Nash says, but gently.

"He'll be beyond excited to embroider something black," Anjali Chachi says. She's not the one on a visit, and the homespun she's wearing looks a bit yellow, a bit frayed. "I'm surprised you bought it, my little revolutionary laddoo."

"It's Japanese-made," Nash says. He is proud of his suit, and I try to imagine him purchasing it, and can't. Nash: wandering the market, alone? I suppose Japanese-made is as good as Indian-made, for the boycott; it will let us sneak a bit of fashion into the wedding. In the canteen after our English exam last year at Bankipore Girls, I'd overheard Mawiyya, Nargis, and Zainab discussing the merits of adding lace to our white saris for a Victorian wedding effect, but my desire to be fashionable does not extend so far as to stray into the funereal no matter how they're doing it in Calcutta. "And it'll be lovely once we embroider it to match Leela's mother's wedding sari."

His mother looks at me. They were friends, I know. "She loved that sari," she says. "She'd be so happy to see it finding a new life."

Maya and I blush and busy ourselves with looking at Seema and Anjali clinking their cups in the British fashion. "The good old days," they say.

"Speaking of older days," Maya says, "might Nash be free to take us around the Shershahi tomorrow?"

Nash raises his eyebrows at me. No, not both—just the one, and I want both to swoon and, simultaneously, to give him a sharp look. I want him to want to walk around Chandrapur's ornate old mosques just for the sake of being in my company.

Ammaji—I still call her Auntie out loud, but I have been practicing calling her 'mother' in the safe spaces of my mind—is still looking at me whilst picturing my mother, and her smile is bright before it falters, and then finds its warmth again. "Absolutely. Maybe this time he'll finally be able to see the fourth pillar!"

It's a silly joke, and an old one—they like to wait until secondary school to explain to us that it's architecturally impossible to see all four pillars at once—but Nash, instead of basking in his mother's affection, is still looking at me. His eyebrow is down, and his face, too, is even. I need more feedback: I need more gratitude. His face is simply neutral, but from Nash, this makes me shiver. I hadn't quite grasped, I realize now, what it would be like to have Nash with me all the time. We made plans, Maya and I, strategies for how to win over each of the aunts, the uncles, his taciturn father; now that we've begun to enact a strategy for winning over Nash, I see I'll never quite be looking at him again. Part of me will always be looking at the way he looks at me.

"Masterji's running late, as usual," Nash says. "Do you mind, Amma, if I borrow Maya and Leela? I want to show them the *Bonsai Gaho*."

"It's in your father's study," she agrees, waving us off.

Though Nash's father's dream is for his son to become an engineer, it's not because he doesn't appreciate the arts: his study is scattered not only with the horticultural magazine Nash has brought back from Japan, but with dozens of similar local prints. There has been an influx of artists since the partition, and those that aren't capturing life in the market and on the streets capture, in painstaking detail, the flora and fauna that surrounds us. Pitaji—I don't suppose I will ever call him 'Papa' if he does manage to force Nash to become an embittered bridge builder—favors the latter. A precise drawing of a gulmohar blossom reminds me of what Nash wrote to me about the bonsai craze—*it keeps me honest,* he wrote, *to realize that to find enlightenment under this tree, I must continue to keep finding ways to make the space I need on this earth smaller*—but when I turn to tell Maya, she is pointedly staring out the window, and Nash stands at my fingertips.

My breath catches. Nash's eyes gleam. "I don't know what I expected, Leela, but…" I think, then, that he will inch his fingertips forward, that sparks will fly. But instead he lifts them up, slowly, my neck, my eyes unable to stop following. He lifts his right hand up above the jawline that makes me sigh, above the eyelashes that make me shudder, until the tips of his fingers are on the top of his head. He closes his eyes.

I am Mohini.

My loveliness has destroyed him.

We spend the week before college begins fostering an interest in Islamic art and writing letters to our old classmates. The less said about the latter, the better. Maya uses our enmity to create suspense—*the project I wish to discuss with you over tea is of such significance as to supercede your superciliousness*—whereas I decide to invite myself over as though there's no reason why I wouldn't want to be fast friends with girls who decided, long ago, that my family's money is my only power. The art bit, for all it's only a front to ensure we're seen regularly and legitimately in our classmates' neighborhood, is much more enjoyable. Nash's father decides that if his son is going to waste a week wooing a girl who's already agreed to marry him, he might as well do it properly, and often when we arrive at a mosque we are greeted by the type of elderly gentleman who is only too happy to lecture Maya about the Mughals while Nash and I study each other. It's not that I'm uninterested in the Mughals. It's just… we were doing fine before them. We were a beautiful, prosperous city.

"Just as we are now," I hear Maya's constant rejoinder inside my mind, as though she's colonized it. I try to ignore both her and Adil Uncle, who has decided to tell us about the apparitions of Quila House as though we have never heard the tale of unreciprocated passion and loss. From afar it seems as though I am spending the last week before

43

college, the last week where I'll not be beholden to a teacher or a mother-in-law, exactly as I'd wish: with my sister and Nash at my side, taking in the sights. It would seem that way from close up, too, I suppose.

"The Japanese would be more interested in Patliputra," Nash says. "Their Buddhist temples are fascinating. Did you know that their version of Avalokiteshwara is a woman?"

"For heaven's sake," I hear my voice and jump at the sound of it. I'd hardly meant to say it in my own head, and it turns out I have spoken aloud.

Nash's brow crinkles, his shoulders fold in to lean over me as closely as he can without touching, without inviting anyone's gaze. At the sight of his concern, my frustrations melt. It doesn't matter what Mawiyya says to me. I will have Nash. Of course, once I have Nash, her old chestnut about the dust of the main road on my house won't apply.

Plus, once those girls get hold of it, they won't want me to be a part of the petitioning anyways.

"Are you all right?"

I nod.

He's not quite sure, or perhaps, dear Nash, he is just conscientious. "Shall we pause for a moment, have something cold and lemony to drink?"

I check to make sure Maya has Adil Uncle's attention, and then whisper. "I'm a bit tired of mosques. Perhaps we could go and get kulfi and sit on the terrace?"

Nash smiles. He has a dimple just on one side, but it's enough. "Tired of mosques, for shame."

"Maya could stay for the whole day, it seems." I smile, too.

Nash drops his voice deliciously low. "What would you say if I asked you to come with me to one more?"

That's not quite as romantic as I was hoping for; still, it's a date. "Of course."

"Without Maya."

Oh.

Once we're married, we'll have plenty of time together. Even, perhaps, plenty of time alone together. After Nash gets home from Prithviraj, and I've helped the chachis clear dinner away, and Pitaji's filled us in on the day's news. After I've finished my teacher training homework, or, later on, put the children to bed.

Oh!

Nash composes his face quickly to mask the fact that it has fallen. "Another time, perhaps," he says.

"I missed you," I blurt out. It's not the logical thing to say, but he seems to understand.

On Sunday a thin reed of a boy comes to our door with a letter. The paper is heavy, thick, lush.

Dear Maya,

How lovely it was to receive a letter from you. I hope you are well, and Leela. I must admit, I'm intrigued. Please come to call next Saturday afternoon at two p.m.; if you might, would you also bring with you the syllabi you receive during the first week of college? I'd like to have both sets, to be thorough. Such thoroughness was how I beat you in exams every year, after all.

Please don't feel like you have to bring anything. I know you haven't anyone at home.

Yours,

Zainab

I am reading over her shoulder, so I can't see Maya's face, but I feel her spine straighten as she gets further and further along.

"Ignore it," I tell her, though I don't know that we can afford to. No one else has responded. Certainly no one has responded to me, and Zainab has only responded to Maya out of a sense of enduring academic competition. Though I anticipate a squirm-worthy hour after which this all dies down, I suppose I do want to follow through. I want to please Nash, even if it means risking the lovely haven that our Hindu college will be. I want to please Nash so that the last invitation was not the last time he'll ever ask.

I know I won't ever be able to say yes; motherless girls can't take risks, and only a fool would endanger their marriage to Nash. But I want to be asked again.

"We have Sonuji," Maya says through clenched teeth.

"You've received a letter insinuating we don't have a cook?" Papa asks. He is on the settee going over his accounts. Business is going well, I think. There is a glut of labor in the countryside now that the Indian Ocean isles have asked us to stop sending them all of our indigent, so labor for the harvests he arranges to be sent to Britain can be had for cheap throughout Bengal. "How odd."

"It's an invitation," I say, quickly. "The Abbasis want to have us for tea this week."

"They have that daughter who was with you?" Papa confirms. I nod. "Seems a bit fast for her to be missing you."

"It truly is," Maya says. I try to will her to take a deep breath by taking one myself.

"Still," I say, "better to go soon before things get busy."

Papa nods. "True enough. Ready for college tomorrow?" And just like that, the conversation turns. We discuss our satchels (mended), our notebooks (fresh and sharp and wonderfully bright), our teachers (thankfully no more Mr. Malik and his infernal droning lectures!), but most of all, our new classmates. The whole reason behind the division was to create more places for trainee teachers and thus, eventually, to create more teachers for students from every Chandrapur community. The twelve new spots for twelve Hindu girls couldn't have been filled by those who hadn't attended high school, of course, but there had been a rush for seats regardless.

Widowed under-twenty-fives would have been given priority, then unmarried over-twenty-ones, and then there would, I expect, be a few like me, who would almost certainly be married by the time the course ends, but who want—whether for reasons purely intellectual or not—to join the educated strata of the city, to be part of this new century. Some we remember as being our seniors at school—Meenakshi Jha, Sweta Agarwal—but others we'll be meeting for the first time tomorrow.

"Maybe they'll have brothers worth knowing," says Maya, folding the letter up and placing it back in its envelope.

I shoot her a look.

"Oh, you can just keep your looks to yourself," she says.

Chapter Three

It's late afternoon—too public a time on the river to get a boat, or else news might get back to the Chowdhurys that their daughter-in-law-to-be travels unaccompanied by either male relative (bad) or sunhat (worse, and I'm already darker than is fashionable). Instead, we sit with our backs to the temple, our foreheads wet with the last of the day's heat. We've set our satchels down—Maya gingerly, me with relief. They are full to bursting.

"What if we're not placed in the same school?" I ask her. The week has been… an education. We've been given lists upon lists upon lists of books that we must read before September, when we'll be placed in classrooms in the nearby villages. Of course, some of them we read at Bankipore, but by no means all, or even most. Getting a hold of the books will be a task in itself; I am lucky I can split the expense with Maya.

But the frustrating part is that we won't be discussing those texts at all. From now until we break up for the rains, no Shakespeare, no Euclid, not even any discussion of the recipes we'd be imparting in Home Economics. We will be discussing how to get children to listen to us, in the broadest sense. The conversations of actual value will happen without rehearsal, in front of the intended audience for the first time. Quite thrillingly, and quite separately from the official list, our teacher Mrs. Mahadev has suggested we add some national and local history into the curriculum, but without talking it over... who am I to decide for the youth of an entire village what they are to know of their past? "I wish we weren't heading out on placements so soon."

"I know," Maya says. She reaches across the satchels and takes my hand.

"I wish our placements were in the city," I say. But the Muslim girls are to be placed in the city, where the elementary schools are still joint. There are more Hindu villages nearby than Muslim ones, and so we are to be split up into pairs and travel

51

into the fields. Meenakshi is quite excited; she says that educating the villagers is what turned the tide for the Japanese. She sounds like her brother's echo.

Most of the riverfront is British estates: green, lush places with the houses hidden amongst the trees. I do want to be like the Japanese; I do want my country back. I know that wearing local fabric, teaching village children English, and asking former classmates to sign a petition is not too much to ask in return for those trees, this river, our future.

"If we don't get the same placement, you can leave after the monsoon break," Maya says, finally.

"That's a good time," I respond, thinking of the wedding. I pull my hand away to pull my hair from the nape of my neck and twist it up into a bun. The sun feels lovely on the newly exposed skin: free.

"You might as well wait and see about the placement," Maya says.

"Of course."

She turns to me. "If we're integrated, perhaps we can be assigned to city schools."

I take a deep breath: it's a river, yet I imagine I taste salt. "It would be good for you to gain experience in a village school."

"Just… try tomorrow. I'll have the rest of my life to gain experience in a village school."

"I'll try."

Maya sighs, too. "I'm sorry you haven't been able to speak to Nash this week. We'll see him Sunday." We were invited to his house for dinner last night, but Nash didn't show. Pitaji said he was at a damn fool café, so we didn't inquire further. I don't know what to do if Pitaji doesn't let Nash pursue something else. Soon enough the British will be gone and then Nash will need a real profession, something where he can be around people, and listen to them, and speak to them, and care for them.

"I miss getting his letters," I tell her. I know it's ridiculous. Nash is lovelier in the flesh than in his letters: his eyes, his desire, his family. But there was nothing about the person holding the pen that I didn't know: maybe there were details unwritten, but those were digressions, the shadows of his life, not that life itself. He told me what he was thinking, how he was feeling. It'd seemed that there was no more to him than was mine, but that, I know, is not so. "On Sunday we'll have something good to tell him, I hope."

"I promise to try my best not to throw Zainab's tea in her face tomorrow."

"Promising to try seems quite weak, when all's said and done. I promise to try not to splash you right now."

"Hey! Try harder!"

Zainab's maid opens the door, and she's wearing a deep emerald green tunic with a peacock blue shawl. I want to turn on my heels right then and there, but when I pivot, I run into Maya vibrating with rage at my back. I take a deep breath and explain that we're here for Zainab.

As she leads us through to the parlor, it's clear that our former classmate's parents—or her in-laws? isn't she married yet?—aren't here. The house is hardly silent, for I can hear pots being washed, bedding being changed, plants watered, but I know that these are tasks that, here, are done by maids and valets. All Zainab has to do is stay beautiful and study, so is it really so impressive when she does?

"They appear," she says to no one, when the maid leaves us at the door to the sitting room. There's tea already sitting out, and sweets that the British call Turkish, but we've always thought of as from Kabul. They are dear, so I take one before I lose my nerve. Before I sit down, in fact, and then I hear Zainab's voice in my head, mocking me for being uncouth, and slatternly. I sit in a hurry, across the filigreed table. Maya takes her time about it, taking stock of the room as though she won't end up just sitting next to me.

Still standing, she says, "You're in pink, so maybe you don't care for independence."

Zainab raises her eyebrows. "I wear white outdoors, where the message is broadcast."

This is all going quite fast. I take another sweet, in case it's all over before I am thoroughly sated. As I brush the sugar off my fingers I see someone else in the doorway: a young man with the same sloe eyes, the same cupids bow. He looks from us to Zainab and then back at us, and then winks, and turns to leave. I open my mouth to speak, but Zainab interrupts. "My brother, Hassan. Ignore him. Tell me: did you bring the syllabi?"

Maya begins to spread them across the table when a thought occurs to me, so I reach across her and gather them back up. "We'll share if you sign our petition."

This is the most admiring look I've gotten from Maya in a long time, and the only admiring look I've gotten from Zainab, ever. "What petition?"

"We want the schools to come back together. It's ridiculous to have two. The British love telling us we'll never be able to rule together, but why should we believe them?"

I'm not met with a witty retort, but she's not dipping her pen in ink to sign, either. I suppose I should have planned out what I was going to say. I assumed Maya was going to do the talking; I guess she'd thought so, too, from the way I can see her canines holding her tongue back.

"Is it that ridiculous? We're training to serve two different populations, and isn't teaching all about connecting with the students? You don't even speak the same language as most of the schoolchildren of Chandrapur."

"Hindi and Urdu are the same," I argue. "How else are we speaking right now?"

She says something I don't understand, and I hear a laugh from behind a door, and then Hassan walks in with a massive lantern. I find myself blinking, and through the rise and fall of my eyelids I see Maya doing the same. "Beg your pardon," she says.

"Pardoned," he answers, his voice throaty. I should have known that he'd be as bad as her. "Stay still."

Why, I want to ask, but neither Maya nor Zainab seem perturbed, and, moreover, they seem to be listening. We sit in silence more a moment, then there's the sound of glass against metal that takes my attention to a box Hassan is carrying.

"I've never had my photo taken before," Maya says, going up to the camera. I take another sweet, but this time, instead of pistachio, I go for the rose flavor. I've heard of cameras, but I don't see the need for them. The Chandrapur School painters are known for being able to capture reality. Is it so important to do it so quickly? What you gain there, you lose in color. And Chandrapur is all color; to depict it in roses, you'd need every variety and then some: an overflowing garden. "How does it work?"

"Ah—no, you can't open that."

I'm looking at Maya and Hassan fiddle with the machinery, so when I reach into the plate and find something definitely not sugary, it takes me a second to remember Zainab. We laugh together as we disentangle our fingers, until we come back to ourselves, and then she sighs. "You really won't give me the syllabi? What if there's something on yours that I need?"

The power I have over Zainab in this moment is more worth savoring than any sweet. "Then you'll have to hope I'm successful in getting the schools to join up, won't you?"

That evening, Maya and I are reading when our guests arrive for dinner; for once, I am reading our schoolbooks, while she is reading a book she borrowed from the Abbasis: *How the Other Half Lives*. I look with her for a few pages, and breathe a sigh of relief that at least Nash does not want to take me to New York. Then Koyal Chachi's visit almost changes my mind. "School again?" she says, when we are clustered around the table, our fingers warmed by the vegetables' thick sauces. "Only you, Varun, would countenance such a thing."

"Yes, yes, Koyal, I know. Sonu, Vikram needs another roti."

"No, bhaiya, I'm completely full," Vikram Chacha says. Then he looks at me and winks, my cue to join him in saying, "Completely fed up."

As Sonuji refills his plate—she gives him a warm roti but also another spoonful of each of the vegetables for good measure—I giggle and Maya groans. We see our father's younger brother far less often than we used to since he took on the Bombay side of the business; unfortunately, when he's away from home, we see his wife a lot more. Goodness knows how my grandparents ever thought they would be a good match. Papa said once, after much begging for an explanation from Maya and me, and a solemn vow on our parts never to speak of what we heard, that by the time Vikram was ready to marry, our grandparents were tired of the whole thing. Though he was only the second son, they'd had enough daughters and miscarriages that they were old even when he was in short pants; their next-door neighbor had been dropping hint after hint until they couldn't be bothered, any longer, to give excuses.

"This younger one is too clever as it is," Koyal Chachi mutters, taking another bite of the potato-

and-pea dish that we serve Chacha every time he visits. "She thinks I didn't see her leaving Pal's Café this afternoon."

The way Papa looks at Maya—just for a second, not even a full glance—I can tell he knew nothing about this, but he says, "That's the entire point of women's liberation, Koyal: she was fetching me an éclair."

I raise my eyebrows at Maya, who is pretending not to see me. Though perhaps she really doesn't, as she's glowering at Chachi as though this is a new point of contention.

"Liberation, vibration," Koyal Chachi says. "Liberation for what? What does she get?"

"I get a life, Chachi," Maya erupts.

I consider interrupting with some update on the wedding, but before I can think of one, Koyal Chachi responds. "Yes, yes, life. But what life? Life to waste on teaching other people's daughters to sing A-B-Cs? Then those village girls can go to further villages and soon the whole empire will be singing A-B-C-D, fine, but then what? Then nothing, and your life has been spent running around children without enjoying their love in return." We are all silent, now; even Sonuji stops in the threshold, her arms sagging under a large bowl of ras malai.

I see that Vikram Chacha has froze, so it's up to me, on Chachi's other side, to take her shoulder, squeeze it, inject it with love. "Maya, knock on wood, will teach her own children, as well," I murmur.

After a moment, I feel Koyal Chachi's posture relax, her breath loosen. "Leela, Maya, you know I love you girls as though you were my own."

"And we, you," I say. I cannot quite tell her we love her as though she were our mother. She may not have ever had children, but we once had a mother.

And after they leave, and the table is bare again, and we are once again strewn about the living room with our books, Papa says, "Avinash's mother will ask you to leave college, Leela, after the wedding. It is up to you, but I hope you do not."

"She won't," Maya says, turning a heavy page, not looking up. "Nash wants someone clever."

"I'm clever enough already," I counter, though goodness knows why. Our visit this afternoon, dinner, they have exhausted me. I should go to bed.

Maya scoffs, and Papa chuckles, and I glare at them both.

After college on Tuesday, Maya wants to go to the market, but when Meenakshi says she already has plans to go with Sapan, I bid my sister tag along with the Jhas. Sapan offers to escort me home first, but it is not on the way, and the sun is still high in the sky, the roads busy with all sorts of peasant women who, though illiterate and, I suppose, unliberated, hawk their wares and carry their tangle-haired children unaccompanied. I should feel terrified, and part of me does, for this is the first time I have ridden alone, and it is only the wispiest whisper of a thought that Nash will be pleased—in Maya's voice, damnably—that placates me. The shade of the carriage is welcome, and the solitude. I have almost fallen into a silent doze when we pass the yellow walls that will soon be mine. I tap on the front wall of the carriage and end my journey a bit early.

It dawns on me as I wait on the doorstep that I should not be flaunting my independence in this way, and indeed, when Ammaji is brought to greet me, she frowns. I am nonetheless welcomed and offered tea, and when I decline Ammaji asks if, in that case, I wouldn't mind if we sit on the terrace, where she is preparing lemon preserves. The smell is intoxicating, and for a while I just sit, blissfully as in the carriage, until I remember I am not alone. "Auntieji?" I ask, for I am not brave enough to claim her as my mother yet.

"Leela beti?"

That she so easily claims me as her daughter makes it easier to bring into words what has been curdling in my chest. "I know you wanted me as your daughter-in-law because of how much you liked Mumma."

She nods while she lays out paper-thin slices, ready for salt.

"Am I... am I still like her, at all?"

The row of lemons grows longer, and another appears below, but the salt will come only when they are all arrayed. Ammaji doesn't smile as she gathers her thoughts, but nor does she clutch each wedge tightly, nor lay it down with enough force to eke out a sound. "Did you know that when she married your father, your mother had never heard of Ram Mohan Roy?" I shake my head, though I imagine the question is rhetorical. "Your father didn't demand a Samajist wedding, so until her

63

own father and mother had returned to the village, she had no idea. Until you were born, your father's little eccentricities were of no concern to her; she was more interested in enjoying city life than forcing ritual on her husband. She wasn't pleased, though, when your father began voicing his dreams for you—she was hardly back from her forty days' confinement when he began to tell her how he planned to show you the office." Ammaji looked up. The lemons were laid; she paused, now, and she mimicked my father's resonant drawl: "'Like Gargi she'll be, but this one's head will be shatterproof.' Leela beti, pass me the salt?"

I do. Sometimes on Saturday morning when I'm having a lie in, I wake up to my father's voice, engaging Maya in some lecture or other, but he's never made me wake up for them. Ammaji continues, "He was quite eager, so Kamini thought she'd better take you along—and Maya, too, though at that point even Maya was still in the womb—and she did, but then something funny happened. At first she'd complain about having to corral you, keep you from disturbing the clerks and the files, but then a new pride entered her voice, and she started to tell me about new investments, new projects. She'd become interested in the office herself. Perhaps you remember."

I didn't. I didn't remember at all. When I thought of my mother, I thought of bright silk and warm milk and the dizziness of having held onto her hands and twirled and twirled. I wished the lemons in front of us were already preserved; I could have used something bold to stick into my mouth at that moment.

"That's why she went along to Bombay, you know. After that your father wasn't so keen on having you in the office, but he couldn't quite pull you out of school... Leela beti?"

I let Ammaji lower me to the ground, put her cool hand on my forehead, wipe away the wisps of hair that interfered with my eyelashes. There was so much I didn't remember... I remembered Koyal Chachi's feeding us porridge for breakfast, and Maya complaining, even then, whining for more honey, but I'd hadn't remembered why we'd been there: Mumma had taken an interest in the business, and gone to Bombay. Where, quite quickly, the plague had taken hold.

She could have caught it even if she'd stayed home, I remind myself, stern as I can. "You must miss your daughters," I whisper.

Ammaji hugs me. "Yes. When you are mine, I don't intend to let you out of my sight."

"You know Sanghamitta?" I ask Maya. She is unwrapping her market purchases, while I am propped up in bed. She holds out a roll of Marie biscuits and I slither forward just enough to grab it. She slaps my hand, takes back the packet, and hands me a single cookie, the little witch.

"Is this about Nash?" she asks, suddenly on guard. She is too quick for words.

Pouting until she proffers another cookie, I look at her purchases. Some of the non-required reading—one on the Bell/Lancaster debate I imagine Zainab will be itching to get her hands on—but most about those ridiculous machines. "Have you decided to become a photographer, then?"

"Don't change the subject," she says, leaving them, pushing me over, and joining me. It's cozy, but this does mean that all of the biscuit crumbs will be on my side of the duvet. "You want to go abroad like Asoka's daughter?"

"It's both about Nash and not about Nash," I try to explain. "Did you know Mumma went to Bombay on behalf of the business?"

Maya breaks off half of the last biscuit and gestures for me to stick out my tongue. The flour becomes tacky in my mouth. "Yes, I did. Papa told me. Did—" She tilts her head. "Leela?"

I chew belatedly, cough a bit. Maya's hand steadies my back. Maya and Papa have always been closer, his rough edges sanding her sharp angles. I look at my narrow feet, awaiting Mumma's shoes. "In the village, they'll be able to tell you how she was as a girl."

"Imagine if they'd had photographs," Maya says.

"Seems a bit lurid to me," I confess. "Would you like your own camera?"

"I think he'll let me share for now." She means Hassan, I suppose. "It'll be to our mutual benefit. He can't take pictures inside purdah, after all."

"And you can't take pictures anywhere else... so we'd better rally up a few more signatories."

67

We look at one another. "It hasn't been so bad as we thought, has it?"

I shake my head, spot the tell-tale glint of foil, and flop over her to open a second round of biscuits. I've got one between my teeth before I remember. "Maya, there's a sugar boycott! These must have been expensive."

"It's all right," she says, waving her arm like a nautch girl.

Her smile is suspicious. "Don't tell me Sapan bought them for you. Maya, please, don't toy with him."

She is toying with me, cramming another sugar-filled disc into her mouth, savoring it as my words dissipate. Then: "'*Today well lived makes every yesterday a memory of happiness and every tomorrow a vision of hope.*'"

Nash has convinced my father that he can escort me to lunch while Papa brings Maya. I, like my father, would never expect Nash to take advantage, but for that memory I've been seeing so often it's seared onto my eyelids. We are driving down the road, but I half expect us to turn a sharp corner and make a run for it at any second. Each time we don't, I deflate a bit.

"I can't believe it's all Shakespeare, Austen, Bronte," says Nash.

"What else did you expect?" I ask. "*The Pillow Book*?"

Nash's face broadens with a smile, but he is taut. "Indian literature!"

We don't turn another corner. "Well, that would fall under religion, wouldn't it? And you can't expect these convent schools to teach the Puranas."

"We have literature that's not religious! What about *The Golden Threshold*?"

"I'm not sure what that is," I admit.

"Naidu! What a woman," Nash says, so openly I am not only aflame with jealousy, but also with indignation. He reddens. "Politically."

I scoff.

"But you're no less," he says. "How was Zubeida's?"

"Zainab's," I correct him. "Interesting. She had a camera. Well, her brother had a camera."

"What, a real one? Did he sign the petition, too? Well, he wouldn't, but what we could do with that camera! You'll have to ask him, next time, to take some photos for us."

It wasn't so bad, then, that I had to go back. "I will," I tell him. Then I decide to continue. "What would you use it for? You and your café friends?"

"To document," he says simply. "To bear witness to our struggle. Think of what the workers in England must be thinking. Our misery under colonial rule has already depressed prices in the rest of the empire—" by this he means the recent stoppage of indentured laborers—"and so imagine a textile factory worker, what they might think, reading about what's happening here. We can't help but depress their wages. We can't help but open the door to exploitation on their very own shores. Why shouldn't they side with us, if only they knew?"

"If only they knew," I echo. There's something to that knowledge-is-power business.

Then something shifts in Nash's eyes. He is no longer looking at me to hear what I'm saying; he's simply looking at me as though he's starving, and I alone am dinner. "If only they knew," says

Nash, and turns off the road, "that we're not going to lunch. We're going to Maner."

"It's all just talk," Nash sighs, as we circumnavigate the crisp, green pools. We are alone, and the mist rising from the water enshrouds us, and Nash is speaking of revolution. "We just sip tea and discuss what they are doing in Calcutta."

I don't know what to say. Let the British have Calcutta—let them have the whole world save this pool, this walkway, the space between us that we have come to Maner to close, that yet remains.

Nash turns to me and takes my hands and instinctively, my eyes close, my back arches—why does my back arch?—but after a moment, I pretend I was just fluttering my lashes. It doesn't matter; Nash is holding me tighter than he has ever held me, but his tone is anxious, his desperation not exactly a mirror of my own. "You'll come with me, Leela, won't you? If we must move to Calcutta?"

I take a half-step back from the boy I intend to marry; it is a good thing he's holding my hands as though they are all that keeps him on earth, because that bond stops me from falling backwards into the pool. "We don't need to move to Calcutta."

"But if we—"

"Just wait for my petition to reach the Directorate, at least." I am already in his hands, and I'm desperate for him not to slip away. The mist is a curtain, shielding us from the eyes of the god who lives in this moss-draped artifice of stone. The memory of my bravery in Zainab's sitting room intrudes, and as I push it away, I pull the bravery from it as if wringing out a rain-drenched towel, and lean into Nash, and kiss him.

I don't know what I expected a kiss to feel like, but what it does feel like first—a deep, enveloping stillness—is enough. I see why Asoka must have pursued this feeling of utter, swallowing stillness so ardently that it reshaped this land. I see why Victoria must have valued her bond with Albert over the experience of total dominion. This is a moment with no rough edges, so smooth, there is nothing to hold onto. I could drown in it and be forever happy.

But Nash takes his hand from mine, and holds me by the small of my back, and our lips smash and lock and draw from one another, and I don't want this to end, either. With my freed hand I put my fingers to his stubbled jaw, pricking myself, sighing with it. He takes another hand to pull me closer, and I run my second freed hand though his hair.

We end it to breathe, not before, and when we open our eyes, I think this might be the best part of it all: to see him, to see him seeing me, to see myself, to see us, and for it to be enough.

As we complete our figure eight around the grounds where, before the stone was laid, Panini walked, we don't say anything more to each other. As we ride back to town, we are silent. Our hands separate as we cross the bridge into town, and by the time we are at the Chowdhurys' doorstep, I wonder if the day has been a dream.

Chapter Four

As the elders scream at Nash—at both of us, I suppose, though only Nash is expected to provide responses—I try to catch Maya's eye. Let them yell; it is their right. Maya is the only one I want to talk to, to divulge not just reassurances but each and every detail. Maya will be the one to widen her eyes when I describe the feeling of touching his scalp, that skin so hidden it will only ever be mine; she will catch her breath when I curve my hand to show her how I cupped his chin. She will, if she would only stop staring at Nash, her eyes obsidian, igneous but silent.

"Don't tell me that children disobey their elders in Japan," his father warns Nash, and I expect the corner of Maya's lips to twitch, as mine want desperately to do. Nash bows his head, but his hands are trembling fists. "You can dilly-dally with your engineering degree for years but cannot wait weeks for your marriage? *Badtameez*," he hisses. Maya! I try to gain her attention through the power of intense glance, to garner a look in return, one that confirms that a bit of insolence seems, right now, to be hugely attractive.

"Come now, Chowdhury Sahib. He's a good boy. A bit carried away, is all." Maya does not even look at Papa, much less me. She is upset, though this adventure should put to rest her fears that I am not taking Nash's new intensity seriously.

"Carried away! Let his shoulders carry away his empty head! Tomorrow I will call Prithviraj and humble myself in front of them, beg them to take my son who cannot seem to finish his engineering degree because he is too busy romancing."

"Pitaji—" Nash's anguish makes my bones ring, but at least Prithviraj is not in Calcutta. I kick my toes into Maya's ankle, but she doesn't flinch, doesn't turn to hear about my own determination to keep Nash here, to keep us here.

"One month." Ammaji's voice is quiet, but we all defer to her. "You have one month to finish your degree, Avinash, and then you will get married and begin your job. If getting married is, indeed, what you wish." She doesn't doubt it, and I don't doubt, either, after today, that Nash wants to marry, but her threat seems misplaced. How will forcing her son deeply and firmly into despair help guide him towards his future?

"Perhaps," I say, too softly to start, so I start again, more loudly. "Perhaps we need not view today as intertwined with Nash's professional prospects."

Ammaji's eyes, when she turns her glare on me, retain nothing of the softness of our afternoon on the terrace. "They are, indeed, better viewed as intertwined with yours." When she turns to Papa, I finally exhale. "Varun sahib, your family has grown extremely modern."

"Leela, too, is a good girl," my father insists.

"You have introduced her to dangerous influences," she says, and this time, I want to look at Maya to make sure she is as furious as I am with the Anglo-Indian woman for ruining Papa's reputation with the Chowdhurys at a time when we so desperately need every bit of normalcy we can project. But she looks pointedly away. "We must be careful who we allow into our family."

"Ammaji, for heaven's sake, leave Leela and her family out of this. I'm the one who organized this, and frankly, all this talk of 'girls' and 'boys' is getting tedious. We are no longer children. I've lived on my own for three years; if we move to Calcutta or London, you'll have to get further accustomed to us making our own decisions."

Ammaji is still looking at Papa. "You've encouraged my son to think of London."

"No," I say, more uncertain than I sound, but what choice do I have? It seems I am by myself here. "We respect you; we look forward to shared happiness. Nash will work towards his degree; I will finish up at training college. After the wedding, we'll both be done. We will have more time, more energy to focus on what is important: family. Forgive us."

Nash's father looks at me, and then he looks to his wife, measuring, I suppose, whether a girl's outspokenness outweighs her contrition.

"Both of you, finish up your school," she says. "It's time for you to grow up."

Papa reads Zainab's note out to us. His voice is still slightly sheepish, but he can't let us have privacy in our correspondence any longer. He has promised Nash's parents that no hint of further scandal will touch me.

Dear Maya and Leela,

Our conversation during your last visit has left me full of anticipation. Won't you call again? Perhaps you might come directly after college one afternoon, books in tow. Let's arrange for Thursday.

As Ever,

Zainab

"That should be fine... right?" Papa ventures.

"Yes," says Maya, even though of course Meenakshi, for example, wouldn't traipse through the streets alone after college to go visiting with Muslim ex-classmates, particularly the Abbasis, whose reputation is itself unclear, outshone in my understanding by Zainab's grace. It's not clear whether I am to aim to be free of scandal altogether, or just return to the base level of propriety that kept me above water before our jaunt.

"Yes," I say, thinking of Nash, and the country, but mostly of Maya. I look at her, but she hasn't looked back since our carriage pulled up to an enraged courtyard full of uncles and aunts, in-laws-

78

to-be, and parents. If I am to be free of scandal, so is Maya. Her remaining days in the city will see her confined to home, school, and tea with girls who just want to rub their sophistication in her face.

"Maybe I should check with Koyal, to be sure," he says.

"It will be fine," I insist, and he assents. And why shouldn't he? Why would I imperil my future?

And he is right that it costs me to do so. My hands are still aflame, days later, with the silk of Nash's hair, my lips with the honey of his tongue. My waist aches without the exquisite pressure of his hands on my skin. If this is marriage...

But. We haven't spoken. "Yes," I've told my father, and I wonder if Nash has heard 'yes,' too, in response to his ludicrous request. I wish, not for the first time, that there was a university in Chandrapur he could have gone to instead, but for that, I suppose, we need to train teachers.

"So you're reading Comenius directly? We've been discussing him through Compayre." After seeing that Zainab has set out the delightful Kabul sweets for us again—she pushes the plate towards me as she pours tea for Maya—I've decided that we can't simply sit in silence. I'm not about to back down completely, but it won't hurt to tell her just what we are reading at the moment.

"Imagine, we could start a chapter of the Comenian Society here," Maya says. "Together." Maya and Meenakshi have already floated the idea of a society branch, though not a mixed one, past our lecturers at the training college, and they have been enthusiastic.

I roll my eyes, but I shouldn't. With Maya not speaking to me at home, college really is the only place I feel like myself. And without snide comments trailing my every utterance, myself has been someone with a bigger mouth than I'd expected. "Or we could just spend that time actually teaching kids." I've taken to pretending I am going to be a teacher, otherwise my head will explode by the middle of term for sure. When I can't bear it any longer, I re-read my notes on our How to Teach Home Economics lectures, underlining anything substantive, to make sure I actually know how to keep house to Ammaji's satisfaction.

"There's one in Calcutta," says Zainab.

"There would be."

"To help us get started," she clarifies.

"We're supposed to be teaching kids to be self-sufficient; we're trying, as a nation, to be self-sufficient," I say. "Why do we continue to see ourselves as a backwater Calcutta cousin?"

"Especially when we're the epicenter of all the surrounding villagers' lives," says Maya, though that's not exactly where I'd intended that thought to go.

"Strength in numbers," I agree.

"But that's just it," Zainab says. "Your whole proposition is based on strength in numbers, ignoring how dangerous that can be."

She's wearing pastel blue today; it makes her skin look positively alabaster. Nargis is prettier, and Mawiyya more charismatic, but Zainab and Maya have always been the smartest, and without her constant companions, Zainab fills the space in the room. What has she ever known of danger, I wonder?

"Imagine," says Hassan in his gravelly timbre, swooping in to take the last lemon-flavored sweet. He shouldn't be here. Last time was a mistake; this time… how do I get him to leave? "The British quit India. Strength in numbers means the end of civic participation for anyone who doesn't think Ravana really had ten heads."

Hmm.

"You!" says Maya. "We were asked to invite you and your camera to join the revolution, too. Though I suppose you're against it? Why're you wearing white, then?"

"Who says I'm against revolution? I'm just against this wool the Hindus are trying to pull over our eyes." He sits down!

"So how would it look, then, after?" Maya asks. I debate picking her up and making her leave, but it's not as though they're discussing anything untoward. I'll just have to make sure we avoid him next time, that's all.

Next time? I give myself a little shake; it's just stir-craziness and sugar, that's all. I turn to Zainab, who's looking at me a little quizzically. I raise my eyebrows at her.

"You're just different out of school, that's all," she says.

"What do you mean?"

"The petition, the Comenius society... you were just quieter, then."

I feel exposed; it's not nice to know that she can see the changes I feel. It was easier to assume she came from a different planet. "I was quieter because you all used to speak over us." I take a sip of tea to ease my internal simmering.

Now she's the one to raise her eyebrows. "We used to speak, that's all."

I sputter. "Nargis used to call me a donkey and bray every time I spoke!"

Zainab has the grace to blush. "Not to your face."

I sighed, and tried to remember: Nash. "Won't you sign the petition?"

"No. I think... maybe we're all better people away from each other. Nargis hasn't called anyone a donkey yet this year."

I place my hand on my forehead.

"Could you bring the Compayre next time you come?" Zainab asks. "I'd like to borrow it, if I may."

I stand up and try to remember how elegantly she's engineered our exit. I'll need these social skills once I'm married into the compound. I turn to Maya, but, as usual, she's left my side without telling me.

Hassan's brought out his camera again, and the two of them are crouched over it in the corner. "Maya," I call, feeling every year of my seniority.

"Same time next week?" Hassan asks.

We are eating litti right outside of our gate, like over-monitored children. Still, the evening air feels soft as we lick the orange filling off our teeth, and the breeze is kind. Calcutta may have a Comenius Society already, but their fried food is infinitely inferior. "I'm glad you're being posted to Kansara," I tell Maya. I've become used to her lack of response, so I keep on talking as though she's responded encouragingly. "And it was nice of them to post us together, as now you've ended up with double the number of students! And Kansara's a fetching town. There's that stupa. Imagine, Maya, thousands of years of ago, Gautam Buddha learned compromise there."

A cow meanders past and I step around Maya to shield her from it; she's always hated animals, even sweet, harmless ones with sleepy eyes. "And I know it's not what we had in mind, exactly, but I'm glad you've been posted to Mumma's village. It'll give you a chance to get used to the place, and the boy, and, well… I'm going to miss you, and knowing where you'll be will make it easier to bear. I can't imagine waking up at the Chowdhurys' instead of next to you, eating rotis without worrying about you stealing the softest one, having a bath without you moving my clothes to the least convenient place." I'm almost looking forward to our tea at Zainab's tomorrow afternoon; neither Maya nor Nash have gotten in touch with me all week, and now that I've realized I want to speak, I've also realized that I want someone to listen. "You'd have had to help me through the placement, imagine. I'd have jumped ahead to the Asoka unit on day one, I have to admit; if the content isn't the point, shouldn't I teach what I want?"

"I asked for Meenakshi."

Empty words are set to tumble out of my mouth, but I reel them back in, and choke on the last bite of the litti. "What?"

"I requested a placement alongside Meenakshi, but they said they'd assumed you and I would want to be placed together. I'd assumed we'd want to spend time together, too, until you went and ruined it all for an afternoon of passion." In profile, my sister's jutting lower lip is hilarious, but I don't laugh. "You have your life to be here, to be with Nash, to teach what you want, to do what you want. Why didn't you think of me?"

I open my mouth to respond, but I don't have anything to say. I realize I've begun to cry, so I close my mouth and wipe my eyes. "I'm sorry," I settle on.

Maya gives me a conspiratorial look, maybe just because she's looking at me sideways on, but then she says, "You should have at least told me what it was like!"

"Maner? We've been there together, remember? After class four?"

"Not Maner, you idiot. It."

By the time my mind catches up to her words, she has unlatched the gate and started inside. I rush to follow her. "We didn't... Maya! You shouldn't think of... that."

She sighs. "Nash did swear nothing happened. Of course no one believed him, but it seems like you are, indeed, a homely chicken."

"Who called me that?" Then I shake my head. "No, I don't want to know. It doesn't matter."

"Seema Auntie," Maya answers anyway. "She convinced Uncle that even if Nash had stripped you down and taken you to a hotel, you'd have" and her fingers become curlicues in the air, "maintained your virtue."

I sit down on the swing in our garden. Pollen swirls through the air around me, affixing itself to everything.

"Would you do something for me?" Maya asks. I nod.

"Would you wait until I'm done with school, and gone? To have a baby, I mean. I asked for Meenakshi, but I was relieved when they said no."

"She's nice!"

I'm glad Maya is at my side, putting her arm through mine. "She is, but..."

"I promise," I say.

I am into my third double-roti when Papa says, "Leela... um. Avinash stopped by my office today. He dropped off a letter."

87

"Well?" Maya says, swinging off her chair to reach for the curd, "let's hear it."

I can't pretend to keep sinking my teeth into the grain, but I can pretend, if I remain stock still, that the world simply doesn't exist. It's not that anything Nash says will be humiliating; it's that, well… "I think," my father says, "that I will refrain from reading it aloud." I look up, and he is looking at me. "Don't tell the Chowdhurys, and, darling, if he invites you to run off with him again, be more discreet." And he stands up, pulls an envelope out of his vest pocket, and lays it beside my plate.

My plate, off which Maya is whisking away the contents. I look at her. "Oh, come on. You're not hungry anymore."

She's right. I hold the letter in my hand—the envelope is Japanese stationary, I can tell by the way it smells very slightly of citrus—and smile.

Though my bedroom must have been mine alone for at least a year, a decade and a half ago, I'm alone in it so rarely I barely think of it as private. It's more of a clubhouse: whereas the rest of the house is decorated in an easy, offhand style with furniture that presumably grew too dingy for Papa's office,

Maya and I have curated each and every inch of this room. The overall effect is more magpie than Mawiyya: a beautiful ribbon from our year seven awards holds back the curtains that were once the shawls from our new Diwali ensembles, a mirror that Koyal Chachi's cousin brother won for us in a darts game at the traveling fair. The bedspreads are older than our attempts at home décor, but while they are faded, they were clearly at one point astonishingly blue; we'd concluded, once, that they must have been Mumma's choice.

I ease myself onto mine without using my hands—they are stroking the paper as if the paper itself was made of skin. Inside the envelope, then, I see the print first—Verma's swinging Mohini, her white sari caught up in the to and fro. When I turn it over, I'm surprised at how short the message is:

My beloved –

Gandhi has spoken: satyagraha! Would that he were at home. Would that we were together. Maya tells me you are visiting the Abbasis each week to convince your classmate to sign the petition. Perhaps you might tarry at their gate a few minutes this week?

your,

Nash

On the other hand, having read it, I feel the need to sit somehow further down. Should I think through it in order? From the edges in? From the clearest to the most opaque? What's most important are the first two words. Nash's letter from Japan had started

My Leela—

Why does it astonish me, each time, to know that Nash sits somewhere, pen extended, wanting me to be his? Why does it astonish me, after Maner, to know that I am loved? Why does it astonish me, after Japan, to know that loving me is just an entryway into raptures about freedom?

I find her sitting next to Papa on the settee, reading a book on, its cover informs, *Raja Musavvir Jung*—by the looks of it, an artist, but not one I've heard of. It's not a dusty work off of a market stall, but crisp; it even smells like a library. I want to ask her about it, but there is a more pressing issue to attend to.

"We're going to evening puja," I tell my father, dragging Maya up by the elbow.

When we're at the gate I remember my newly constrained circumstances and, instead of calling a carriage towards the river, drag her down the road to our local shrine. Chandrapur has been growing so quickly this past year that I don't recognize half of the crowd that's gathered to chant the verses about Hanuman, the loyal monkey. We hang at the back and, when I don't say anything, Maya begins to sing along. I elbow her in the gut, partly to get her attention and partly simply because I am furious. "You've been writing to Nash without telling me?"

She shrugs and stops mid-line, inauspiciously right in the middle of a verse explaining that whoever either sings or listens to the story will reap a mountain of blessings. "I was trying to help. Meenakshi said Sapan told her Nash has been acting strangely lately. Presumably he's disconsolate."

"How is hearing from you going to make him less disconsolate?"

Some newcomer to the neighborhood with a ten-year-old boy in tow glares at us, so we sing a few verses, and then I see the roasted corn seller turn the corner. I lead us there in no hurry so we end up at the back of a line, and feel foolish. We could have had this conversation at home, not surrounded by listening ears.

"Leela, wake up! He sets up this romantic day for you, and then you tell me nothing happens, and then you just settle back into his parents' punishment... He needs to know we're working on the petition – that you're fomenting revolution, if not romance. Nash isn't the same boy who used to chase us with red dye at Holi!"

"You're right. He's the one who'll be my husband unless Ammaji and Pitaji catch you passing notes like children! It's time to grow up, Maya, and stop trying to turn everything into an adventure. Some things you have to handle with care—"

"Ammaji and Pitaji? Already?"

We couldn't be closer to home, yet I'm acutely aware, at that moment, that I stand outside the gate. She shouldn't have meddled, but Maya's stricken face as she runs back is my own doing.

"Lime juice?" Anil asks, holding out the corn.

"I need to go," I tell him.

This time, we go to Koyal Chachi's. Vikram Chacha is away—this time, he's down in Cochin.

Chachi does most of the cooking herself, though she has her help make the rotis. He smiles at me as he puts one, still puffed, on my plate. Though he's only a few years older than us, he's been with them for years, and part of why Koyal Chachi secretly hopes that revolutionary fervor will die down is that she doesn't want him to run off to re-join the Birsaites. "Imagine," he laughs, "Miss Maya off to the village while I enjoy life here!"

"Kansara's very beautiful," I argue. He is tribal, so I think his village is farther to the south, closer to Ranchi. He spends one month a year there himself, but generally in the winter, when the relative lack of dust makes it easier for Chachi to be without him.

"I'm looking forward to seeing it myself," Chachi says. Dinesh is about to put another roti on Maya's plate, and Chachi swats his hand away. At least in the village they don't starve girls into litheness—I think. "Will you be coming back, Maya?"

"What do you mean? Of course she will," says Papa. He is nursing a whiskey, rather than eating; he has a dinner he must go to, he's told us, but with a careful choice of words, never explicitly blaming work.

"Oh, so in this there's no woman-gets-to-choose?"

"Choose what?" Maya asks, taking the fresh roti I've just been given and tearing into it before it can be whisked away.

"I just thought you might want to simplify, to move there properly. The principal of the school will surely hire you right then, and you can get married. Simple."

"Don't be silly," Papa says, standing up and putting on his hat. "Have a good night, my favorite ladies."

"Papa?" Maya calls him before he's quite out the door, and he turns. "It's my choice, though, yes?"

He steps back in the house, and starts untying his shoelaces. When he's barefoot again, he walks back through the front room to the table where we sit. "Maya, what is this?"

Another roti has been laid on my plate, but it deflates, neglected, as I study my sister. She doesn't quite sound cheerful enough for the question to be rhetorical, but she's not said anything to me about leaving school. I can't imagine her anywhere else, yet. "You wouldn't leave, surely?"

94

"No, no. I just wanted to check that my life was mine to shape."

"Of course it is," I assure her.

Papa is quicker to connect the dots than I am. "Maya, I know this engagement would not be your ideal choice, but it's done. And Sagar is a good boy."

"Sagar could be a Wright brother, but that's not the point, Papa. What will I do in the village?"

"Do?" Koyal Chachi asks. "You'll be a teacher, you'll be a wife, you'll be a mother—trust me, you'll be busy."

"Just like here," I echo. Sometimes she is right. Papa nods.

"Just like here," Maya says, but with a sigh.

Chapter Five

We get to Zainab's early, at my insistence, and go straight in. The scene is the usual one: she sits on the divan, deceptively delicate, with the sweets on the table in front of her and the stray tweets of a forlorn maina bird coming from the direction of the kitchen. Hassan is nowhere to be seen, but thankfully his camera is set up in the corner, drawing Maya like a moth to flame. I take a deep breath and pull my chair as close to Zainab as I can without drawing Maya's attention. "I need a favor." She can send Hassan out to tell Nash that I still adore him but must set an example, but will she? I am starting to think that without Mawiyya and Nargis, she might be relatively kind. Or, if not kind, acquiescent in her loneliness.

She smiles. "You mean besides this?" She reaches behind her and brings forth, like a magician, a scroll.

I unravel it.

We, the undersigned, hereby petition the Chandrapur Directorate of Schools to integrate teacher training colleges for the educational benefit of all.

And the signatures:

Mawiyya Khan. Mehrunissa Khan. Nargis Begum. Farzana Ali.

I look at her.

"Are you going to thank me first, or jump straight to asking me why I've not signed it?"

In my hands, the paper is heavy, the words hold weight. I feel something unexpected well up inside of my heart: pride. "Neither," I say, standing up slowly. "Excuse me a minute."

I leave the room with padded steps, thankfully not colliding with Hassan, who is lurking in the living room doorway. So long as Maya thinks I'm just using the commode, I should be all right.

Really, I'm sure the news would reach him soon enough.

But... Nash is steps away, and I'm holding the first thing we've made together.

I've forgotten about the maid, and she asks, understandably, if I'll need a carriage or my shoes, or if I've lost my way. It doesn't matter. Outside the gate, I realize I have no idea where he will be. Or if he's come at all. And then I realize how visible I am, my head uncovered, alone. I should go back inside, leave the balmy afternoon behind, thank my hostess. And then there Nash is, leaving his bicycle under the margosa tree at the corner, surprised and pleased to see me.

He's not sure either, I can tell by the way they rest upon his pockets, where to put his hands. He doesn't lean in to embrace me, and he doesn't, even in whisper, call me "beloved." But he smiles.

"Look what I've got," I say. I unroll the petition, holding it gingerly from the top. He takes the bottom, our elbows casting interlocking shadows over what I recognize as Nargis' flowery script.

He laughs. "Leela! You're a marvel."

I glance up at him, and catch him glancing down at me. The bottom of the scroll curls up into the air as his hands find my waist. Are satisfied and ravenous really opposites? I feel both. I tremble. "See? We can change the world from within our world itself."

"You can," he says, and I will change seven worlds, change them into diamonds and dust, if his look of admiration follows me to each of them.

"Leela?" Zainab's voice floats into my ear, and I jump. She is at the door, looking like a bhoot come back to life. "Who's your friend?"

I turn to him, but Nash is righting his bicycle. He winks at me, waving as he zooms away. "Sorry," I tell Zainab. "Just a friend, passing."

When I reach the door, she cocks an eyebrow and grins. "Just a friend, passing?"

Back in her front room, we sit on the same side of the table, nestling up with a sweet in each hand, the scroll by itself on the seat to which I'd become accustomed. As I whisper to Zainab about Nash, I try to keep hold of the feeling of his hands at my core. "But," I find myself saying, then stop.

"But what?"

I glance at the scroll. She's brought it up with her friends, even though she doesn't agree. "I'm worried about him. He seems to think that freedom fighting is a good alternative to engineering, that they're equivalent."

"It's a risk," Zainab agrees.

"Yes, and — well, he asked me if I'd consider moving to Calcutta."

"Obviously you know what I think."

I sigh. "Why are you still here, Zainab? I mean, you're rich, you're beautiful, you're educated... why haven't you married someone who'll take you where you want to go?"

Zainab looks like she might respond, then shoves a sweet into her mouth. As she chews, she looks at the scroll, too. Finally she says, "I was, almost. But it's over."

This week I barely pay attention to the lectures on Modeling Behavior. I should be listening, if only to do my duty towards my placement students, but since I have promised to leave school my body floats above the classroom, bestowing bemused glances at the serious girls with their plaits and their well-starched whites. There is no point, either, thinking about more colorful saris: the boycott, instead of winding down, seems to be revving up, and this train of thought takes me to what I want to linger on, anyway: Zainab's Tragic Past. Papa receives the newspaper every day; at present, they are awash with explanations and opinions about Gandhi's understanding of the value of truth, which is ironic, as it seems they conceal as much as they report. Had the Sinhas known, when they housed the two up-and-coming politicians who served as excuse for the lavish Diwali soiree four years ago (I had just been told that Nash would be my husband, and that he would soon be leaving for Japan, and had remembered the confusion and Rooh Afza tastes comingling on my tongue the whole night), of the Chandrapur plot? Why hadn't the papers reported its undoing at the hands of a rookie cadet?

"He was relieved to be free of the cantonment at night," Zainab had told me. "His was a rowdy barracks, and we had been besotten with one another since childhood." So that was what did it, I thought, that's what gave her the veneer of glamour: context. She'd known all along that grace was as important, seen as moreso, as quick recall of Gupta-era trivia. "Manning the gate was mostly a matter of staying awake; who would try and get caught up in mischief near racks and rows of law-enforcing young men?"

Perhaps Hassan had heard the edge of wispiness that had crept into her voice; I hadn't realized he was there at all, but now he led Maya away from the camera corner and sat watching his sister's inimitable composure falter. "That the conspirators were discussing their plans for the coup in his earshot was mere chance: negligence, really, on their part. But when he realized they were actually going to bring the Nepalese king in to establish a Hindu regime, he had to act.

"He wasn't acting for the British, or against the Hindus. He wasn't like that. He was simply fighting for a just country.

"The British might have let him out with a caution, but for his Hindu barracks-mates, it had gone too far. Reporting a Hindu plot to destabilize the independence movement? We're used to it now, but back then no one wanted word of that to get out and inspire people."

Zainab had grabbed my hand, then, squeezed it like a sister. "You see?"

I thought I could, but since, every time I manage to let my mind drift away from lectures on how to encourage childhood sanitation or stop children from using their left hand to hold the chalk, I see more. I see that Saturday afternoon that Nash took us to the Hanuman temple; had any of those soldiers been asking for forgiveness for their role in her intended's disappearance? Perhaps they were glad to see him gone.

I see that Friday—Nargis had mocked the henna Maya and I had so carefully applied in anticipation of our wedding days, calling our handiwork backwards, our hands themselves rough from making our own beds. Maya had laughed, in return, when Mawiyya mixed up the Maurya and Gupta dynasties during the question-and-answer session. I'd felt wretched, but now I feel wretched thinking of him, even more outnumbered, even more than indignant—frightened, and right to be so.

And then—underneath it all—I wonder if I should feel a thrill of triumph. Didn't we get him? Didn't we summon up our strength in numbers to chip away at centuries of rule by the few, the rich, the proud?

We have dinner at Nash's on Tuesday night; neither of us mentions the petition. A few times, Nash tries to ask me how college is going, but I let Maya answer.

"And how are your studies progressing, Avinash?" my father asks, cutting Maya off as she explains how we are to threaten to rap on girls' knuckles if they forget their blue books on exam days. "You'll be able to take up the job at Prithviraj after the monsoons?"

Nash swallows. I immediately regret my earlier coldness—it stemmed from confusion, not disregard, but how is he to know the difference? I've entreated Papa several times to convince Nash's father to allow him to do something else, anything else, but on this matters his usual affability fades. "And what would you have him do?" he asks, and to that I have no answer.

It seems Nash has been doing some thinking of his own, however. "I am on track to receive my degree, yes," he begins, "but I've also corresponded with scholars in Calcutta about the possibility of attaining a legal education. When independence comes to Chandrapur, we will need leaders with a strong background in jurisprudence."

"Like Gandhi," Maya says.

Nash smiles, even though Maya is the only one looking at him with anything like encouragement.

"Like Gandhi," he agrees, and then he turns to me, "or Asoka. We won't have to put up with Edward's pale imitation forever."

"Such lofty dreams," Nash's father says. "And how do you plan on funding this legal education? And where? Japan is closed." *And we are out of money,* he doesn't add, for our benefit. But I am thinking of what Nash has said. What Gandhi is asking us to do seems simple-minded; our white saris and promises not to lie won't get the British out. The Chandrapur plot—to bring in a strong, Hindu king—seems like it offered better odds, but... something in me has shifted in the last few weeks. Nash is right to bring up Asoka. But his father laughs, now, trying to bring our conversation back to something that complements the korma. "So don't worry, Leela. Avinash will still be here, and ready, for your wedding. Though of course whether the tailor is ready or not is another question."

"Well, I'm sure he'll manage," says Ammaji. I smile back at her, instinctively, but wonder: what if Nash manages it? A law degree? Another future?

They are careful not to leave us alone, but as Maya and I leave to sit with the women in the front room while the men remain at the table, Nash gets up to walk me across the room. "Is everything all right?"

How can I say either 'yes' or 'no?' "I miss you," I say, insufficiently.

Nash seems unsure if that is all I mean. "I miss you, too," he says. His voice drops. "Maya no longer brings me news of you. And the petition was such a surprise—an amazing one, but, Leela…"

"There is so much we have to talk about," I say.

"Can I visit you on Thursday? At your friend's place?"

I look at him. His eyes pull me, two broad, deep magnets. "We can't. I have to be an example for Maya, Nash, can't you see?" Getting the words out is like grinding sandalwood.

He glances back; Maya is walking behind us, carefully not listening, but shielding us from the others' eyes. "Isn't it a bit late for that?"

We are at the doorway, but I daren't step through it. "What do you mean?"

He opens his mouth to speak, but he can't. We are children in spun sugar, here, stopped in time, like our nation. "I will get you a message," he says, finally. Then, after a pause, he adds, "my beloved."

The next day after college, Maya and I think to walk on the riverside—we can't risk a boat ride—but it's so hot that we duck into Padri ki Haveli, the tall, cool British church. We duck into a pew like the convent school girls, but we can't bow our heads: the roof above our head soars, and we can't help but contemplate. Though perhaps not what we were meant to contemplate: I wonder just how the convent school girls concentrate with a semi-nude man hanging from their altar. He is gaunt, to be fair, and smooth, like a plucked chicken.

We don't often come here, but we nod a quiet hello to the priest and then are not disturbed. I point out the cracks in the wall from the 1857 Rebellion, before even my mother was born. "Soon it will be the 50th anniversary," I muse.

"Leela, you're happy we're putting forward the petition, now, right?"

I look at her, instead of the cracked wall. "Aren't you?"

"No, of course I am. I want us to be a part of this movement."

"I'm certainly happier about it now that I won't have to suffer the consequences," I begin, but I don't want to turn the conversation towards my leaving school, even if it does mean I get to escape even the shadows of my former tormentors. "I want to be part of the movement, too." The church is so quiet, moreso than a temple would be at midnight, and I think back to the opening of a Japanese poem Nash sent me, months ago: *along this road/ goes no one.*

"Sometimes Meenakshi goes to the café with Sapan," she says, and I bring my mind back to her. "You know, where they all gather? To plan?"

"What are they planning?" I ask immediately.

She shrugs her shoulders, looking for all the world like an American actress, the pew her stage. "They've asked me, again, to bring the camera."

"I think Zainab keeps purdah." I am doubtful she'd want to go, anyway, with that cumbersome machine. "Hassan would have to bring it alone. And, then, he might not need your assistance."

We sit in silence for a few moments, and I wonder if this boycott, the '57 revolution, all of this is just theatre. Surely the British will never really listen to us, never really leave us. For the paled-faced amongst those who pray here, Chandrapur is their home, however poorly they treat it. "Maya, something

Nash said… do you think you can ask Meenakshi to find out what they're planning?"

"You wouldn't ask him?"

"I will…" I feel for Nash, throwing himself into thoughts of this disharmony day after day, when his fundamental nature is so good, so loving. But don't I tell Maya all the time to adapt to her future? Why can't Nash simply finish his degree and let the others play the game of rebellion?

It's no longer because I think his happiness depends on it, I realize, though I do think so. It's because I'm starting to understand how the slender, grasping fingers of the very thought of freedom turn from a thin creeper on a young tree into a vice. I finally let myself see what Maya will see in Kansara: a vacuum. I do not want Maya to leave Chandrapur, ever, I admit to myself. In her fight against segregation, I will help her; in her fight against the British, I will help her; in her fight against her marriage, I cannot lie and promise, in a church, that I will help her. But I will do my best to make sure she is okay.

The messenger from Nash also brings a gift: a thin box containing a pair of small silver prongs, cherry blossoms carved into the head. The note accompanying them reads:

My beloved—

When I bought these hairpins, I wanted to present them to my bride, to symbolize that which our marriage will hold together. But, Leela, you have taken on more than your share of keeping us whole, and I apologize. I should not have let Ammaji wrest you from school.

In Japan, young men who have been to war enjoy their share of glory, but, Leela, make no mistake—they have returned deeply changed. For fifty years, Britain has refused us a war; instead, they carve us up like they do their birds, small, carefully labeled pieces perfectly sized to be eaten. What we must do here, we do with the support—and this I promise you—of the entire Indian animal. But I am afraid of what will come from thinking of ourselves in this way: as animals that must, if war is not waged against us, bring it forth.

Aurobindo reminds us that India rises not to trample on the weak. Gandhi centers non-violence. I want to hold these close to my heart, as I do the memory of the feather softness of your hair.

> *your,*
> *Nash*

Papa and Maya are discussing whether we might buy a gramophone, and for a moment I consider pulling Maya away, to the terrace, perhaps, or simply to our room. But Papa smiles at me, and beckons, and I go and sit with them and show them my new hairpins.

"He's thoughtful, your Avinash," says Papa, and ordinarily I'd smile at the phrase 'your Avinash,' but right now, my heart hurts.

"Thoughtful," repeats Maya, running her fingers over the finely-wrought blossoms, "and with excellent taste."

"Yes," I say, but it comes out flat, and they look at me.

"Goodness knows," says Maya, echoing my tone, "if you'd ever be able to imagine life without him."

Oh, Papa. Of all the nights to not be sneaking around! With no other way to approach the riddle, I take her question at face value. "I don't think so,"

I say. I think back to the message, wondering if I am missing hints that Nash has decided, without me, that we will be going abroad. No: if that was what Maya knew, she'd be upset. "No matter what he does."

"I wanted to be a doctor," Papa says. "I'd hate to be an engineer, too, but it's nice to work with your Chacha. Nicer than I'd expected when I was begging your Baba to let me go study sciences instead of commerce."

Maya gives Papa a proper hug, then, throwing her arms around him and squeezing. "Oh, Papa," she says, but she is laughing, and I laugh, too, and throw my arms around them both, and my heart feels all right, for a minute.

Maya has passed the petition around to our classmates; the response is divided. Although the camaraderie that developed when Maya and I weren't speaking hasn't dimmed, Meenakshi and Maya find themselves each defending their position during our lunch break. While the rest of us unpack tiffins, Meenakshi explains why the split benefits us the most. "The new places. The greater attention in the classroom. We would be mad to fight on principle for something that would hurt our younger sisters, our neighbors, our cousins. Let's leave politics outside the classroom."

"The classroom is political," argues Maya.

"Is that something you'd have been brave enough to say during your lunch break at Bankipore?" Sheetal asks, and we all know it's a rhetorical question. Sheetal has already signed the petition, so her interjection seems oddly timed, until she adds, "What better practice at gaining authorial voice than arguing our case to the Directorate?"

"Exactly," says Maya.

"You need to remember that they've signed it, too," Meenakshi argues. "So don't be naïve: what do they think they'll gain by being with us, those privileged Chandrapur princesses? They just want to seem progressive."

"I think," I venture, "they might really feel afraid, and alone. "

Everyone looks at me, and I feel like a real teacher for a second. "They feel more powerful to us, but in this country, they're greatly outnumbered. When we get our freedom, we'll be in charge."

"Exactly why we should get practice leading," says Aastha, a quiet woman who'd been tutored up to and after her betrothed was run over by a carriage. "Or the men will just mess it all up again. Have any of you heard what they're planning?"

We shake our heads, all of us… except for Maya. I widen my eyes at her, and she looks down.

"There are reports of riots brewing in Dacca," Aastha says, "and my brother says there's discussion over whether that's good or bad. All of their Gandhimania is just talk. If we'll have the power, we should be prepared."

No one responds. Apart from Maya and Sheetal, no one has signed yet! Mawiyya will certainly want to take charge of this henceforth, and if there are more Muslim signatories, I don't know that I'll have the grounds to object.

I straighten the column of white cotton that has made its way from farmers to weavers to merchants across the subcontinent onto my body. "If we have the power, we should be prepared to work together." *Leela Chowdhury*, I sign. "Next week we'll join with the girls who've signed from the Muslim college and set up a meeting with the Directorate. All of you, even those who haven't signed, are welcome."

I steal a look at Maya, hoping for a smile. I get one, but it's shaky. We gulp.

"And so by keeping expectations raised until the final day—even the final moment—of term, you encourage students to use the breaks as a period of consolidation, rather than of departure from, the material. These *School Days* excerpts—thank you, Seema, yes, do pass them around—are interesting and enjoyable, too. Let Tom's days inspire your students to aim for the Cambridge certificate; why not?"

I didn't have to raise my hand, as Meenakshi said it first, unprompted. "Or to Japan. It's not like English is necessarily best anymore, is it?"

I don't know why we're giving Mrs. Dvivedi a hard time; it's the final day of school before monsoon break—short this year, just a week before the others are off on their placements—and she's wearing her homespun, as she's worn every day this term, with a no-nonsense pride. Still, the air is so hot as to be oppressive—if it didn't happen every year

115

I'd never believe there is to be rain any day now—and this makes all of the other oppressions of our lives more leaden. Plus, instead of eating laddoos afterwards, Maya, a few others, and I are walking across the grounds to the Muslim school to meet our counterparts, and then together to the Directorate.

"Well, yes," Mrs. Dvivedi says, not disagreeing but doing her best to get us back to whatever she feels she must tell us before we're off. "The oldest, at any rate."

Maya looks at me and grins, and I can't help but oblige her. "Mrs. Dvivedi," I say, unable to simply speak without being invited yet unwilling to wait until she calls for questions. She nods. "Certainly you can't mean that. After all, we're sitting here in the epicenter of ancient Indian scholarship: Nalanda, Sompura, Varanasi, Telhara…"

"The point is to inspire them," she says. I have never exasperated a teacher with my cleverness before, and I enjoy the tingle in my fingers it produces. Is this how Maya and Zainab feel every day? Perhaps I should do more of it, I consider—and then freeze. It's too late to think like that. This is it: my last day. When Nash found out he was to leave Japan, he wrote me a letter in which he told me that *the world feels a smaller stage for my emotion, today, than the entire earth; how can that be the case? It seems the line between my fingers, my brain, and my heart will never survive this severance.* I had never fully acceded to the stage, I realized now, and it would be forever too late.

"May we try to inspire you?" asks Maya.

"Haven't you already been trying?" Mrs. Dvivedi grumbles, but she waits for it. Last year, this is when Mawiyya would have whispered a snide comment just loud enough for everyone short of the first row to hear. Here, we wait for Maya to go on.

"After we let out today, several of us are going to petition the Director of Schools to cease the separation of teacher training colleges." Those of us going smile at one another, but I can't be the only one nervous.

Mrs. Dvivedi raises her eyebrows, her face otherwise a cipher. "We're living in the new century," is all she says, and then she turns back to the lesson.

When we finally wait for the Muslim girls at the entrance to our old building, I find myself wishing that Zainab were here. Maya and Sheetal are giddy in the fresh air, pulling the shawls of their school uniform tight against their busts as the male students pour out of the college buildings. I frown, but as we're not standing near a food kiosk, no one bothers us. The scroll seems too light in my hands, and I clench it against a nonexistent wind.

"Oh, there they are," says Sheetal, waving at the palanquins, pointlessly unless they are peering through the slits at the side of the curtains. She breaks off from us to walk ahead, glad to be reunited.

Maya pulls my palm from the petition and gives it a quick squeeze. She gives me a glance I'm only just getting used to, waiting to see if I'd like to be the one to speak. She must have based her decision on my trembling chin, for she takes the lead. Nargis and Mawiyya expect it; their minions stand in their shadow.

As they descend from their regal perches into the Directorate lobby, I've forgotten how beautiful the two of them really are. Though Mehrunissa and Mawiyya are actually sisters, it's Nargis who seems to be the Snow White to Mawiyya's Rose Red. Her lips are full, her nose is straight, her skin seems to be that of a girl who only goes out in the moonlight. Mawiyya's beauty is more frustrating, in that her looks are closer to mine, but an improvement upon them. No one would call her dark skin dull; its smoothness sets off the sheen of the strands of hair that escape from her scarf. Nargis' white garb makes her look like a British bride, a lost princess, but Mawiyya's beauty belongs here. I feel myself slipping into a familiar superfluity.

I've completely missed Maya's pronouncements, but I don't ask for her to repeat them as we make our way into the office. Instead, I bring up the rear and try to ignore the way my stomach clenches.

I do not hear braying; I don't.

My tears are falling into still-hot tea as we cluster in the parlor.

Maya puts her arm around my shoulder. "It's okay, Leela."

Sheetal, standing somewhere beyond my tears, says, "You were great, Leela."

"Oh, give it a rest," says Mawiyya. I wipe my eyes clear for that, though honestly, why? "Sure. We may have had a good idea, but we knew we were wasting our time in order to give Leela and Maya

119

fifteen minutes to feel less like idiots than usual. Merchant's daughters, you should know we should have had our fathers with us. Brothers. Uncles."

Maya and I give each other skewiff glances, guiltily. We wanted to impress Nash; we have impressed Nash, up until now. But we've pulled our classmates into it, too, and I wonder what it must have cost them. I don't, I must say, *care* if Mawiyya and Nargis are in trouble with their mothers-in-law, but Mehrunissa and Farzana and Sheetal I feel more kindly disposed towards, and it's Farzana who speaks next. Her voice is softer than I remember, but firm; she's never been one to prevaricate. "We've talked about this, Mawiyya. We must be paragons of self-determination."

Mawiyya would never do something as inelegant as roll her eyes in the Directorate parlor in full view of the secretary, but her voice takes on a distinct grumble as she says, "Self-sabotage."

Nargis sighs. "Let's get out of here. He's waiting at the main gates." She means Anis, her husband, who sent her a huge, English bouquet of roses last February. They were wilted, though, having been sent for from Calcutta. In Patliputra, roses grow wild where Asoka's wisdom fed the soil.

Sheetal gathers up the cups, and we begin to smoothen our hair for the walk – short, but with boys lingering over snacks on each side of the wide alley—until Maya speaks. "Let's ask him, then. Anis is respected. Perhaps the director will be convinced."

"Are you sure?" I ask Maya, though he's not her husband, and Nash is not hers to impress, either. I'm not sure myself, but I'd forced myself not to let Mawiyya usurp me, and we've ended up just where she expected. It's just—Maya's not one to give up what she has.

She bites her lower lip as she sneaks a glance at me, but when she looks at Nargis again her voice is firm and she speaks as though she's been saving the words for the right situation. "Yes. Self-determination is noble, but we must be determined to achieve our ends, not just to try."

Mawiyya looks at Farzana, raising her eyebrows, but I imagine Farzana could burst into tears right now and it wouldn't make any difference. She doesn't, and Nargis says, "All right. Wait here." She takes Mawiyya by the elbow and they leave us. We've been tea-less for about two minutes, but Mehrunissa has already pulled out her embroidery.

"Off they go," Sheetal says to Farzana.

"Off we go," Maya says, to me.

Though we needn't pass it, not quite, on the way home, we have the carriage stop at Patliputra. I need to walk these shady boulevards, imagine a world where the pools were full, the courts full of wise men.

Maya has been silent, and now, when she speaks, I am not surprised at the vitriol in her tongue; I feel as tangled up by the day, as slick as a greased wick. But I am surprised when she directs it at me. "So that's you gone, then."

"Don't say that."

"Oh, Leela. You've left school; do you think you'll not let him convince you to leave town? Even Papa wants you to go."

"But—"

She clasps my wrist. "I'm not stupid, Leela. I know it would be better for you—Nash will do well, given a bigger audience."

I shake free of her, upturn my face to the weeping willows; they ground me, but still I feel perilously close to throwing my innards in the air, letting them take flight. All this school, sold to us as an equalizer: that which will fill in the crevices made from youth, and swarthiness of skin, lying in wait for a baby I want—I do want—but can't yet imagine. All this school, preparing us to speak, and I have done my part to prepare Maya so well that when she thinks of my future, she thinks only of what it portends for Nash. "I'm not going anywhere, Maya." I want to say more, but my unpracticed tongue fails me. Instead, I throw my arms to the sky. Let Maya laugh: let them all laugh.

She does not. After a moment, I see her own arms join mine: we call to the Sun God, progenitor of our lineage and that of Asoka. After that, of course, I see her sloppily-tied pallu slip off her shoulder and onto the dust of the path. It would be salvageable if she wasn't wearing white. I lean to pick it up, and I redo the pleats before folding it over her shoulder and tucking the loose end into her petticoat. "I wish you were staying here longer,"

I allow myself, finally, to tell my sister. "You'd do well with an audience, too."

There's no call for humility between sisters; she nods. "I'll have one, though, regardless: my classroom. But, yes: as long as we remain here, the city is ours to liberate. Forget petitions: we must do something powerful, and soon. Something that tells the Directorate, and everyone else, loudly, clearly, that segregation will not stand. That partition will not stand!"

Oh, her lovely bluster. She would be aggrieved to know it calms me. I lead us back towards the carriage. "Of course change must come soon, but let's not forget the petition quite yet: it may yet bear fruit."

Maya raises one eyebrow. But she says, "of course," as we emerge out into the hot sun.

Chapter Six

"So that's it?" Zainab says, taking a rose-flavored sweet, bright against the sea-form green cotton of her chemise.

"They'll keep us in the loop, surely?" I don't know why I'm at Zainab's today. As we ate breakfast this morning, finally free to wait for the monsoon from within the confines of a shady room, Papa asked us what our plans were. He hasn't taken holiday this year. Usually he does, during the school break, and we'll make the trek to my mother's village, but there's no time. Ammaji has decreed that our wedding must take place before Maya goes to Kansara; no one but Papa, it seems, is sure she will return. And so what seemed so far off is now so close I cannot picture it clearly; it shimmers, like one of the Monet paintings Nash insists owes its beauty to Japan.

Papa told us not to wait for him for dinner, without clarifying that he was busy at work; I suspect a dinner with the Anglo-Indian woman, but I neither ask him nor suggest as much to my sister.

Zainab hmphs, and then says, "We'll keep you in the loop, make sure you know what the Directorate decides." She means her and Hassan, who is sitting with Maya next to the camera as always—it's too late, I think, to tell him to disappear, too awkward now. "Your sasural must be excited with this new Lal Bal Pal initiative."

So caught up I've been in the last week of college and the Directorate meeting that I've barely given any thought to my in-laws-to-be. Lal, Bal, and Pal, our three revolutionaries, have been more in the forefront of our minds as we claim our own small stake against partition; Nash's Gandhi preaches truth, but these three are responsible for our boycott, which I think is truth in a form more sublime: we wanted self-determination, and the boycott shows the British, and not only the British, that it is possible. Now they've called for non-payment of taxes, which I am less sure about. "Excited about the prospect of arrests? Of riots?"

"Of a bit more money in the coffers, at least."

"We've plenty of money," I say, though I wonder. Might it be enough to give Nash the legal education he wants?

"We don't," Zainab says. "I don't know what we'll do if Hassan doesn't marry well."

We look at our younger siblings. They seem not only younger, but newer, somehow, engrossed as they are in the machinery. "Might he not?"

Zainab sighs. "No one has money. Just you lot."

"That camera seems expensive," I say, but what I mean is, "just like this house." The neighborhood we sit in is leafy, the compounds here built both to last and to adorn. The British section of the city is undeniably beautiful, with the houses buttressed by colonnades and ringed by placid lawns, as though our street had been swept of people and pulled long and wide like taffy. When I was a child I wanted to move there, but the past few years have shown me the folly in that. Where Zainab lives, the windows look out over the river, but they sit shuttered, and instead of inviting the viewer to look out, they bring light in through an intricate net of triangles and fleur-de-lis. Zainab would think of our house as one for getting out of, and she wouldn't be wrong: it's a base from which we go to work, to college, to the temple, one day to the club. Hers is a place to nest in. It's no palace, but Siddhartha himself might have found it an effective shield against the truths of the world outside.

She nods. "Its presence here has been a matter of some disagreement. My father isn't exactly against him using it to document the boycott, but he'd prefer he dispatched someone else to take the actual photos. He even asked if the maid could be taught to use it."

I wait a second to ask, "Could she?"

Zainab giggles. "Hassan threw such a tantrum at the idea of any one of us putting our sticky fingers on it." She looks at him, and then back at me. "It's a wonder he's letting Maya touch it."

"She's not that clumsy," I assure her, but I don't like it either. She needs to be preparing for Kalsara and beyond, where the new century is still a thing of the future.

I am surprised to find Maya at the gate on Thursday morning—she isn't the type to pray before breakfast, after all—but we all act strangely in the still days before the rains come. Papa, for example, hasn't eaten dinner with us all week. One night might have been suspicious, but he can't possibly have been eating dinner with that woman every night, right? I think of what Zainab said; we are doing well, and won't the new movement effectively be a tax refund? Maybe my father has long yearned to spend some more money on her.

If I had money, would I send Nash to Calcutta? Or would I figure out a way to use it towards the movement and thus convince Nash we should stay here?

It is a matter best approached delicately, so I lure Maya into the kitchen under the pretense of perfecting our sev recipe before the rains come and make us crave it. When Sonuji gets an unexpected break from the kitchen in the middle of the day, she prefers to take the time to travel to the market near the new houses surrounding Nala Road, where her niece sells gourds. The house is empty, then, but I still can't quite say it. Instead I wait until she is up to her hands in dough and start with, "We should get my trousseau finalized."

She doesn't turn around, just says, "Let's wait until later."

"If we realize we need anything, it'll be easier to go sooner rather than later."

"I'm not saying we have to go to the market in boats."

I wish she would turn around, but I understand. "Maya… it's time."

She turns around then, slowly. "Fine."

Her face is inscrutable. "Fine?"

Oh, now it is simply irritated. "I said fine. Let's just go now."

I quickly blow out the gas on the stovetop. "There's another reason I think it might be prudent."

She has already swept past me, almost through the narrow doorway. Behind her, I call, "Papa might have cause to look through it soon himself." Maya turns, her long plait tracing an alif on the dusty walls. I say it, then. "That woman, she…"

To be quite honest, I have no idea if Papa has ever looked in Mumma's trousseau. For reasons more emotional than logical, we have simply assumed he hasn't. He's not prone to fits of grief or other maladies befitting a widower, nor does he have such a keen eye for fashion—not to say that he is ever underdressed—to want to reminisce simply about the clothes. He has his memories, and we have a box of silks. It seems fair to leave us ours. I can't stand the thought of Papa looking at her, dressing her.

She mightn't want them, of course; she's Anglo-Indian, not precisely British, so it's not as though she hasn't any proper clothes of her own. I suppose we haven't had as much to do with that community as Papa has, through his business; I wonder what will happen to her if, instead of putting us back together again, the boycott leads to further and deeper partitions, or indeed if the revolutionaries get all of their dreams come true and the British quit India altogether. I picture her in Trafalgar Square wearing our mother's sari, one of bottle green shot through with silver, but the setting in my head is black and white.

It's from a photograph, the square is, I realize, from a postcard Meenakshi's uncle sent her and she brought into class in the third form. I'm not sure I like having my mental pictures mechanically supplied. I color it in in my head, but I'm not sure what color her eyes are.

Maya shrugs. She shrugs! "He'll miss us."

"How dare you!"

"How dare I think about the future? Some of us have to."

"Not everything gets to be about your going away!"

"But… I am. And no matter which saris I take with me, I'll be alone, Leela. I don't want Papa to be alone, too."

I'm tearing up a lot these days, but I can't help it, and Maya comes back to me to squeeze my shoulders. "What if we look at everything, and there's nothing we want to leave for her?"

"You choose first, then I'll choose, and then we'll see." Which means Maya will absolutely leave something for her.

Which means Maya has given up her chance to choose first for her, a stranger.

Maybe I've been a better example than I give myself credit for. "All right."

"Come."

Now that we've found ourselves at Zainab's without any hope of movement on the petition, Zainab's asked us if we might finally show her our syllabi—"desegregation," she suggests, "at the one-to-one level." Maya and Zainab pore over one another's papers as I nibble at my sweet: since Zainab has admitted their financial difficulties, I try not to scoff them, as I'd really like to do.

Hassan comes and sits next to me for a change. For a few seconds, he joins me in watching our sisters and nibbling, then he says, in his gruff voice, "Some bad news for you, girls. Anis got a written reply from the Directorate. No luck."

Maya and I look at one another and sigh.

Then Zainab says, "A written reply?"

"Yes, you know, *we've respectfully considered your proposal* and all of that. They said public opinion on the matter had already been adequately surveyed."

"Oh, so now they respectfully consider it," Maya says. I don't say anything, just let the slow burn of indignation fill me.

"Mawiyyah and Nargis had to plead for a week to be let out of the house for that meeting!" Zainab says, just as indignant, and it pricks me. We are the ones at her house now, aren't we?

"It's not right," Hassan agrees.

"They have no idea what we can do," Maya says, more darkly than her comment deserves, for what can we do but petition, and petition again, and I suppose take photographs? Maya would make a good photographic subject right now, I think suddenly: with her eyes rimmed red with fury, she's not a Ravi Varma type, and she's too softly built to be a Chandrapur School peasant—but just as she is now, she strikes me as beautiful.

Not beautiful, I amend: worthy of record. "Hassan," I venture, "would you be able to take Maya's picture right now?"

He studies her, and in that pause I wish I hadn't asked. If he says no, now, perhaps Maya will feel worse. "In the garden," he says, finally. He gestures to her. "Come."

I get up to follow, but as I pass her settee, Zainab pulls at my snowy pleats. "Wait, Leela, can I ask you something?"

I sit.

"You and your... friend," she says, smiling just with one corner of her mouth. "The one with the bicycle, the freedom-fighter," she clarifies, as though Nash could be anybody else, and I nod. "Is it nice?"

"Well, yes," I say, but I am happy to say more. I quash down the part of me that wants Mawiyyah and Nargis to come and see me now, the voice of glamour, because I don't want my happiness with Nash to mingle with the smaller parts of myself. "He's always been so thoughtful, even before he went to Japan, and then while he was there he wrote, religiously, and—"

"Leela," Zainab cuts me off, her voice mild, but her posture determined. "When he kisses you, is it nice?"

"Oh!" I look at her and smile out of one corner of my mouth, too. It's nice to have someone to talk to about this. "Zainab, I can hardly describe it. His lips are rough, but somehow they feel almost magnetic. And then—" I stop myself before speaking about Nash's tongue; my goodness. And in that quiet moment, I realize that Zainab isn't just a not-Maya. "Oh, Zainab, I'm sorry. It's not..."

But it is, so I don't continue.

135

"I sometimes wonder if I should seek marriage again," Zainab whispers. "I've spent such energy coming to terms with being alone. And then—the classroom is enough interaction, isn't it, for an average day? And then... I'm muddled, Leela."

"I think," I say, carefully, "the kissing part will be—would be—nice." I hold her secret, and it feels like a jewel in my palm.

"But children?" she says. "We bask in our rebellion, but freedom will not be kind for us, for... me. These may be children of another father, but I don't know that they will be spared violence."

Violence. My indignation today has stemmed from the absence of a letter, just a slight thing. But, of course, such slights gather, and Zainab knows this more than I. "Nash spoke of violence."

I am chilled, then, so drastically I think about Maya outside and wonder how much longer she must pose. I want to drag her back into the sun, across town, to our terrace, where violence appears only in newspaper reports of foreign wars.

Zainab sees the change in me, and she doesn't push. "Perhaps your petition will have been enough," she says. "They may reconsider, with time."

"Of course they won't," I sigh, though she was only trying to help. "But there must be something to do in between another useless petition and the riots everyone thinks will be next. And I want to do it." It's my turn to whisper, and I'm glad we're alone here, Zainab and I. "Everyone speaks of Calcutta and London as though they carry their own power. I think that perhaps we can take advantage of that, as students, as girls. What if I wrote to Edward?" I have been thinking aloud, but as quickly as I have turned my shiver of fear into one of excitement, it dissipates. Asoka himself would be as likely to respond as Edward.

I wait for Zainab to say something cutting, but instead she says, "Not Edward, maybe, but we went to hear Lord Curzon speak last year in Calcutta. He railed against diploma factories, and he sounded like he sincerely does care about what type of education would be best."

"But everyone hates him." The viceroy's plans were often ridiculed in the political cartoons; they thought his plans to overhaul the school system to get rid of cram schools would choke the levers of mobility that allowed us to reach parity with those whose white skin afforded them what ours didn't.

"Mumma and I were in the closed carriage, but I thought his manner of speaking was quite charismatic. And he's the one with the power, isn't he?"

We stare at one another, and I feel alive.

We're at Nash's for dinner, and though we're all in our proper white, my mind is on a taupe and violet georgette that would have been perfect for tonight: the official night of my engagement. We'll be the first of the season, and as such, Ammaji is determined to set the bar high. As we're served small bowls of black, buttery lentils, she explains that everything without a preordained color (like the orange marigolds) is going to be green and orange. "Nothing red, white, or blue," she says, "our own small nod towards independence." I think of the letter I spent three evenings writing, and asked Sonuji to post this morning, without telling anyone—even Maya.

"Lovely," says Nash's father. "And have we decided on the menu yet?"

"First course khaja, second course malpua, third course balushahi," says Anjali Chachi, and we all laugh. It'll be a sweet enough affair, but we'll need some savory food, too.

It's a happy argument with the smallest of stakes, so we all dig in and try to persuade the table; it's the perfect occasion, then, for Nash to meet my eyes. I haven't seen him in days, and the very instant makes my back arch. What I would give for a wink! As Seema Chachi makes the case for jackfruit, I wonder if my mother had ever thought ahead to my wedding. She must have, right? In just one week I'll have plenty of time to ask Ammaji. It seems I've been waiting forever, but now it's just enough time to whisper my farewells to each room of our house.

After dinner, Papa arrives, apologizing for a busy day. We've all settled in to listen to Pitaji play the harmonium. He's talented, his forearms strong, his fingers nimble. I hardly listen, though; Nash has snagged a seat beside me.

Probably, we could look at one another, and no one would say anything. It would verge on rude, but we might say a few things without being scolded. I try to catch his eye, but Nash is looking

139

quite deliberately ahead. I swallow; I've been so busy being joyful, tonight, that I've forgotten that the boy I'm marrying isn't quite the one who'd left.

He came to me first, I remind myself. He took me to Maner.

He'll be upset, though, when I tell him of my failure with the petition; revolution, to him, seems to have become almost priceless.

Almost, I repeat.

I nearly jump when his right index finger finds my own, traces a short path down my nail. A mistake, perhaps. But when he does it again, his finger rests at the tip of mine. I push back, heightening our connection, and when I steal a glance at his face, he's broken out into a smile. Maybe, I conclude, things will be all right.

The dreams that follow from the tip of Nash's finger wake me, thirsty and restless in the moonlit night. I push my eyes shut to give myself back to them, but the city's panoply of sounds makes it impossible. I ease out from under the sheet—the raindrops could be boiling as they fell and I would still need a sheet to feel fully ensconced—and look across the room. Maya sleeps like the monkeys made to dance on the road to the villages; she'd never be that jerky awake. It's been awhile since I asked her to get me a glass of water, and even longer since she's agreed instead of laughing herself back to sleep. Plus, if I speak to anyone else, the remnants of these dreams will shrivel into the night's shimmering heat. Anyone but Nash, of course, but he might as well be in Japan, for all he's a few streets away.

I pour myself a glass of water from the jug Sonuji leaves outside the kitchen, treading lightly so as not to wake her. In the living room, the light streams through the cracks in the shutters bright as the beams from Diwali lanterns. It's so hot, and the rains so imminent, the lizards have gone into hiding, taking to shady niches under stairs and beside the water tank on the roof.

On the roof: that's where I'll see the moonlight more clearly. That's where I can look out over the city and let its noises complement the whispers of desire that the night has brought from Nash's lips to my ears. With each step, I remember one moment of our kiss at Maner. I want Nash, I know that—I have known that for years—but there is nothing

141

familiar about the way his kisses have made me feel. I stand at the edge of the flat roof and want to step off, certain that if my body were to act the way I feel I would fly. I look in the direction of his family's compound, where on the roof clothes hang from the line, suspended in the windless night. Underneath them, a figure stands, and though it is too far to judge, I know it is Nash.

I want to be alone with my betrothed.

I could wave, perhaps, and call him towards me, and then run and open the gate for him as though I were simply early for the milkman. But I feel the memory of his arms around my waist and feel pulled towards him.

Last week I finished my education. Were I not a queer, motherless girl, I would be a woman already. By my own measure now, I should be ready for what lies ahead. Yet here I stand, waiting: for the night to end, for the rain to fall, for the viceroy to decide to respond. For some things, I must wait. But Nash feels mine, and until marriage makes our touch an obligation...

I run down the stairs, only the tips of my toes gracing the smooth, hard floors, and slip through the gate, pretending to latch it behind me, hoping the moon will discourage thieves or rapscallions from testing its truth. The sweet moo of the cow nestled into the space between our house and the alley makes me smile, and I know that though this is not how Mumma might have imagined it, this is how I will become a woman.

The streets are not empty; a city of Chandrapur's size and honor bustles whilst most of its citizens are abed. Any other year, my white nightgown would have the street sweepers, the deliverymen with bicycle-wagons full of fish and fowl and fruit, the mouse eaters gape; instead, I float as though in a sea of ghosts.

"Are you all right, miss?" asks a woman with pan-reddened teeth and a village accent so thick I lean in to make sense of it even as I recoil from the scent of rotting jasmine that surrounds her. An opium-eater! Perhaps. But when I nod and rush forward, she does not follow.

The cane seller usually camped out at the college during our lunch break has taken up his trade at the corner of Nash's family compound—the whirr of the wheel seems to have attracted the night watchmen of the area, as several men in line are holding batons. Our eyes meet for a second, and though he looks away without a sign of recognition, a heaviness creeps into my toes. The worlds of the night people and the day people are not so impermeable; I could easily be seen. I may have already been seen.

In that case, I decide, there is no point not proceeding. I am not a homely chicken, I tell myself—and then I see a familiar face in the cane line: Nash's night watchman.

If Maya were ever to find out about this moment, I think, as I catch my breath and duck past the shadowy fence that guards the extended family as they sleep, she will never go the village. But Maya is not long in my thoughts: Nash's compound is a rambling old building, but one I know well, and I am soon caught up in skipping steps and avoiding tiles I know will belie my presence as I make my way up to the terraced roof. To the wuthering heights I go, I whisper to myself, though I know their roofs are slanted, and the air is as far from wuthering as it is quite possible to be.

The thought of Nash's touch has just fuelled the most outrageous journey I have ever taken,

144

but for a moment, when I first see his silhouette against the low, wide moon, I cannot move. He is so beautiful, so warm; as the rings of smoke from his cigarette catch between them the invisible beads of the night sky, I wonder if I should wait, just a moment, just for him to turn around and cast his arms around me.

He stiffens, aware of my eyes on his neck, and I don't. I don't wait. I close the gap between us, and, as he turns, I take his chin my in hand and pull his lips to mine.

We pull apart at the same time, but Nash regains his sense first. "Leela! What are you doing here? Are you ill?"

I giggle. "Do I look ill?" Although then I consider the question myself: I'm in my nightgown and slippers, hair undone, and though the heat is oppressive I'm shivering. "I'm not ill. I just saw you from my roof and, well… I wanted to be with you."

A hundred expressions flit across Nash's face, shock and scandal not excepted. But then he lets his widened eyes half close again and says, "My little

Majnu! I couldn't sleep for wishing you were here."
He is committed to the sentiment, not the words—the
latter half of his sentence is half-swallowed by his
own kisses. I reciprocate. My feet have wandered
half across town, and so I give my hands permission
to wander, too; through the thin cotton pockets of
his pyjamas, I feel the differences between us.

I am trembling as Nash pulls me closer to him,
closer to… well, closer to parts of him I've seen
only on the holy men whose naked dips in the
Ganges wash their mistakes away. He is firm, hard,
throbbing: all of the words I've rushed over in the
Mills and Boons tales of Outback ranchers and blue-
eyed governesses. I should've read more slowly; I
should've remembered what to do next, because
Nash is pulling away, with a lack of surety in his
eyes I want to quell. "Nash?"

"Leela," he says, his voice thick, unmeasured.
"I don't know."

I've come so far to touch him, and when I take
my hands back into my sleeves I feel further away
from him than before. "About me?"

He turns to me so fast, the ends of his tunic spin, his eyelashes flutter. "No—no! I... you enrapture me. Just, well, what if we're found out?"

I'm so relieved, I laugh. "If anyone was going to see me, they would have already seen me." I want to place my hand on his back, but not without permission, so I lift my arm up, slowly, but he intercepts it, and takes my hand in his. I lean towards him. "I've been thinking of Maner. I've been thinking about what we didn't do then." The sky is behind me, the city beyond, and yet Nash's eyes are full of me. "I'd like to try it now."

Nash closes his eyes before he responds, so I stare at the copper skin of his eyelids. "Your sister... she told me you made a promise."

It's my turn to close my eyes, but only because everything I've done in the past hour has come rushing back to me, coated in her likely response: giddiness, horror. I wish I could slap her voice from my head; right now, to be honest, I wish I could slap her. "She told you?"

"She said that since it involved me I should know about it..." Nash squeezes my hand. "Leela, open your eyes. It's okay."

We look at one another, and laugh. "You're going to marry a madwoman," I admit. "I just… after we're married, we'll have time alone, but everyone will know. I just wanted something for us, something just between us."

Nash is silent a moment, and then he says, gingerly, "If you come with me to the city, our lives would be entirely between us."

Thousands of people might point out that Chandrapur is a city! "Nash—if we're struggling for self-determination, shouldn't we stay close to the very heart of who we are?"

"But, Leela, in Japan—I realized we're part of something bigger. Even if, even when, we leave the Empire, there's so much to be done, not just here, but everywhere."

So much still to be done: I wonder if Maya, in her infinite communications, has told him about the decision of the Directorate. I suppose it's nicer not to have to tell him that we were ignored, but it's as if he doesn't even remember. I don't tell him about my letter. "Here, too."

The sound that leaves Nash's throat is halfway between a sigh and a sob. "I know, Leela. But wouldn't you rather be listened to elsewhere than ignored by those you thought were yours?" He taps his toes. "All I do here is sit and talk about wires and bridges and it's turning me into someone you'd be afraid of."

I do place my hand on his back, then, and let my slow, soft strokes temper his hastened breathing. "I'd never be afraid of you, Nash."

He shook his head. "You'd leave."

"I'd never choose to leave you. You, this city— you're my future." His breaths have slowed, but I leave my hand on his warm skin, snaking it upwards towards his neck, kneading the muscles supporting his shoulders. "Maybe we could think about petitioning the Directorate for a professor of law, so that we could do the course by correspondence? I know it's not ideal, but now that they've agreed to let Prithviraj act as sponsor for your engineering degree I imagine that they just need to be presented with a plan backed by someone important. Your father, maybe."

"We?"

I pause. I hadn't planned to say it aloud, hadn't planned to say it even within the confines of my own imagination. "Teaching is not for me, Nash; it never was. But if I could stay here and study more… I think, maybe, I might want to spend some time figuring out what justice is." I am blushing, but, the flush of my cheeks hidden in the moonlight, I feel brave enough to ask, "If they don't allow me to take the course, maybe I could look over your materials?"

Nash was smiling broadly now, his teeth like stars closer to home. "You might," he said. "There's a woman called Cornelia Sorabji who was appointed to the Court of Wards last year. I think she must have her law degree, to do that. I'll show you the article they ran about her in *The Telegraph*."

"Sorabji." I let her name escape through my own teeth. She was Parsi, it sounded like: upper class. Were we in school together, she might have laughed at me as a motherless merchant's daughter. But maybe not. And maybe it wouldn't have mattered.

"Nash! Nash!" I grab his shoulders with less fluidness in my limbs than I did an hour before. This time I'm trying to unsettle him, wake him. The moon is still up, but the sun has emerged, too, and the city I recognize—and more importantly, recognizes me—will soon be out and about. "I have to go."

He jumps to his feet, then, seeing me, sits back down, but doesn't take me back into the crook of his arms. Have we really slept entwined, Romeo and Juliet sans tomb? I am alarmed by the possibility of discovery, yet weighted down by sheer happiness. Nash's hair is unkempt, and he looks, if I can dare to say it—delicious. Stern, though, as he plans my escape. It's not too elaborate—rather than try to evade the watchman, Nash will bribe him to deliver me home and keep our secret—and then he tells me, "But be careful en route, Leela. I should have sent you back as soon as you arrived, but... well. Be careful."

"It's morning now," I point out.

He nods. "But there are riots brewing."

"In the east," I say, but I think of what Aastha told us. In Kansara, at least, Maya will be safe. As I nod, I feel something—a fat drop of rain, right on the tip of my nose. "Nash!"

We grin at one another, exhaling just as, I know, the rest of the city is exhaling, those awake and

151

those whose breath is released into the closed air of their bedrooms. "You should get going," Nash whispers, but instead of readying himself, he leans forward and kisses me where the rain has just been. I still myself, a willing canvas.

A raindrop falls on his ear, and then another one, and soon the sky is emptying itself upon us. In a moment, we will run down the stairs and I will endeavor to get back into my bedroom before my nightgown clings too irredeemably to my legs, but for now, we close our eyes to the rain, and we kiss.

When I get back inside, Sonuji steps out of the kitchen to watch me drip onto the hallway rug; instead of saying anything, she fetches me a towel. I dry my face but not my hair, planning to wake Maya up by shaking my head on her face so that she can wake up to the good news. I rake my tongue against my lower lips, anticipating her shrieks of terror and then delight.

Maya isn't in bed.

Perhaps the rain has woken her up, and she's on the roof. In fact, she might have woken up with the sound of the rain, found me gone, and assumed

I was on the roof. For less then a moment, but more than no time at all, I regret missing the last morning I will ever have to usher in the monsoon with Maya. I suppose last year was the last time, then. We hadn't cared at all about the future in those days, in most ways, though Maya'd been angling to have me "hand her down" my turquoise-and-silver shawl as Koyal Chachi had gotten me a new one—red and white damask—as a Teej gift. Koyal Chachi was strange about gifts: she was thoughtful enough not to simply get us two of everything, but she never understood Maya's taste. That year she'd gotten her a bracelet; we'd gone later in the week to have another link added.

It's like her to leave the bed unmade, and I go to smooth the sheets before heading up, so I'm facing away from the door when I hear footsteps and the pitter-patter of monsoon drops mediated by white cotton sari and disheveled hair. "You have kohl tears," I tell her, tossing her my handkerchief.

Wait.

"You weren't on the roof, either!" I pull her to the bed—we're getting her side of the bed soaked, not mine, at least—and she's fidgeting, trying not

153

to grin. "Maya, you shouldn't go out at night! It's not safe!"

I would have dabbed my eyes, but Maya pushes hard, though precisely, where the kohl-blacked rain had left its traces. "Don't worry," she says, airily, "no one saw me."

"Don't you *don't worry* me," I tell her. "There are riots brewing; you know that. What if...?"

Maya rolls her eyes. "You're soaked. Did you go to the roof?"

I stare at her for a second. I'd come into the room wanting to tell her, but...

She's taken my silence for assent and stands up to begin unwrapping. "Hold this," she tells me, handing me the end. I roll it around my hands like a muff as she spins slowly.

"Maya, where did you go?"

She's unhooking her wet blouse, and I unsheathe the pillow to hand her its case as a towel. As she dries her underarms, she says, "If I tell you, I can't un-tell you."

"What does that mean? Maya, what have you been up to?" I start to think through time periods where I'd not been with her. There were those weeks

154

we weren't talking; even apart from that, I suppose I've been going over to the compound more, for fittings and just generally to get in Ammaji's good graces, even if Nash is never there. But mostly we've just been together, right? Reading a load of pontificating about what it means to teach village children their alphabets?

She stares at me, naked, straight-backed. "Hassan and I are in love."

Chapter Seven

I take three steps forward, again. And then a fourth, and a fifth. I'm past my father's door now. If I decide to go in and tell him about the danger that Maya is putting herself in, I will need to make the conscious decision to turn around. Unless, that is, he's heard me and comes out into the hallway of his own volition. I have been pacing for the last ten minutes. It's still early, though, and it's been years since we've intruded on father's privacy before breakfast, years since we needed to crawl into his bed to evade the monsters under ours.

I like Hassan. I like Hassan! I mean, what I know of him: he's quite good-looking, I suppose, and he has a camera, and a beautiful house, and he's from a family respected by his community despite a recent dip in income. He sees no problem with his sister getting an education, and he agrees that the British should quit India.

But that's it. That's all I know about him. And Papa knows even less.

"It's not like Papa and Nash are best friends," Maya had said. "Papa doesn't know he won't end up being a madman." She'd looked like she was biting her tongue.

"But he knows that their family does not have a history of producing madmen," I reminded her. "And he wasn't just told that. He's seen it, and before that, he has his father's memory, his grandfather's memory, and so on. I'm not saying that anything is wrong with Hassan, personally, but how can we trust him or his family?"

"Because they're Muslim?"

"No! And put some clothes on. Tell me he hasn't seen…"

"That's none of your business, you hypocrite."

For a moment I thought she was talking about my sneaking out to see Nash, but she meant the projected anti-Muslim sentiment. "Maya, there's nothing wrong with being Muslim, but –"

"Cosmology aside."

"What?"

"How can there possibly be just heaven or hell, and that's it? I'm not converting, if that's what you're afraid of. I'm not even Samajist, for all Papa's proclivities. I know that's old-fashioned, but still. There's no glamour without ritual."

"Maya, people are not going to accept you."

"So?"

"What do you mean *so*?"

"So... no one accepts each other, here. We don't accept the Muslims in our school, they don't accept us in theirs, the Directorate doesn't accept ideas from girls, the British don't accept ideas from Indians..."

"Don't be ridiculous. This isn't politics. This is your life."

Maya pulled on a nightgown, white. She didn't have to say it. Instead she said, "It's not like their acceptance would have meant anything to me in the village."

I left her then. She didn't care that she'd be able to come back from the village, during her confinement and for the odd holiday and just, if she wanted, to see me. She didn't care that riots were brewing and it wasn't just about turned up noses, but slashed noses, red blood splashed on homespun. She didn't care that she was putting my marriage at risk, my father's business, our home.

I've been pacing, but I don't know if telling my father will do more harm than good. If I help her with this charade, at least for the time being, at least until my wedding is over... I could help her hide it. She's done it so far.

No, I can't. I turn. I knock.

"Maya darling?"

I was here first, I protest, but not aloud. "Leela. May I come in?"

He knows this isn't going to be a lighthearted chat, so he shuts the door behind him. I sit at his vanity; he perches at the end of his bed, briefcase at his feet as though he'll rush to work if things get messy. Before I know what to say, he says, "I expect this is about where I've been spending the evenings, and I'm sorry I've left it so late to explain that it's upset you."

"Oh," I say, because actually, I want to know. Is he about to confess to a love affair, too?

"On a few of the evenings, I've been talking to Avinash's father. I've been requesting that he uses

159

your dowry for the boy's studies in jurisprudence in London."

I stand up and turn towards the window in case the nausea that has risen up within me will express itself in actual vomit. Papa clambers up and puts his arm on my shoulder. "Leela? Beti? I thought this is what you wanted!"

I can't even look at him. If I focus my eyes on the bullock cart laden with melons, by the time it has made its way down our street, I will shake my head to find out that none of this has happened.

"Nash has been quite vocal about his dislike of the engineering profession, and I suppose I thought your... recent enthusiasm conveyed support. And even before that—before his trip to Japan, even—you were always talking to him about books, walking with him through all the historical sites; it was part of why I've been so satisfied with the match."

"Walk with him through all the historical sites of Chandrapur," I murmur, and he cocks his head, but I don't repeat myself. In London he will never hear me.

"Anyways, it didn't work," he said, and I spin around so fast I see stars. "He wouldn't even agree to the University of Calcutta, not that I have any connections to see him placed there. I felt bad. I had been working up the courage to tell you."

I stare at him. "You should have told me before you made the request in the first place."

He looks a bit crumpled. All of a sudden, I realize he's not as young as I remember. I feel a rush of tenderness, but it's fighting the ebbing nausea, the overarching tightness in my bones. "I'm sorry," he says.

"I should go," I say, though it's the monsoon, and I've told Nash I'd stay at home. In the hallway I consider going back to Nash's house anyway. I can't share my worries about Maya with my father, but after the night I should be able to share anything with Nash. Though—perhaps he already knows, in which case he's felt he can't share everything with me.

We long for the monsoon, that excellent excuse to stay indoors with a bowl of something hot and crispy to eat; now that it's here, I stare at the deluge outside the window, wishing it were clear so I could go back to where I'd spent the night. If Nash knew, and felt he couldn't tell me, even though he'd mentioned news from Maya before, it meant he agreed with her. Even though he'd sometimes spilled his own secrets, he'd never spill what he thought was hers to protect.

He'd agree with her; I know it. He doesn't even know Hassan, but he'd be happy to see Maya marrying a revolutionary and my reminders that the real world still exists would be cruel reminders of a cruel world. There's no point calling the carriage around for that, so instead I gather my valise and sit on the divan with some stationary and a fountain pen, and the words are easier to come by than I'd thought. *Dear Zainab...*

When Maya chews her cauliflower at dinner that night, her lips are exaggerated, her manner sullen and defiant. I can't look at my father without feeling tears pool in my eyes, so I stare back at her as she tries to assess whether or not she should tell Papa everything. He is quiet himself, hopefully feeling guilty, but it makes the house seem more motherless than ever. We keep to our own plates; we keep to our own thoughts.

Until Papa says, "Maya, there was a letter from your Mausi today." Our mother didn't have any real sisters, but he means Anamika Mausi, her second cousin and Sagar's mother. "I'd written to her about your placement. She is thrilled to have you in town. You'll be staying with her, of course, instead of in the teacher's home."

He sounds matter-of-fact, rather than resolute in the face of scandal, but Maya isn't quite sure: her eyes widen, her fingers full of potato freeze in midair. It isn't until she opens her mouth to confess that I hear myself cut in. "Of course," I say. "She must be excited to have a chance to get to know Maya better—and then she'll have a whole two years to anticipate her return. I wonder if they all wear white in the village, or if there shall be some relief there." Maya stuffs her mouth, but as she swallows, she slouches, breathing more easily. Should I have told? Writing to Zainab has calmed me down, somewhat, the physical act of transferring my anxieties to the page, but it brought no resolution. I want Maya to be happy without ruining our lives; I know my father does, too, but I don't know exactly what

163

shape he will want that to take, or if he will even think it is possible.

"As one likes, I believe," Papa says, and I wonder if we will all sink back into our dinners, but then he continues, "but I should tell you this: Mausi asked you, Maya, to marry at the end of the placement, and stay in Kansara. I told her no. She may be a tad upset."

Oh, our dear Papa! During the moment of silence that follows, I try to use this news to recalibrate my hopes, my expectations, and my path forward. So far, his indulgences have cost him nothing, but it seems he's willing to be understood as more than eccentric—as uncooperative, even. My surge of pride, though, is coupled with hesitance. He is not my little sister; he is my father, and he must have some self-preservation; he must. If Maya confesses, and in response he cancels Maya's wedding entirely, word will get back to the Chowdhurys, who will supply their own explanation—thankfully, I'm sure that whatever they imagine will be better than what is actually the case. If Maya does not confess, Mausi may continue to insist—but Papa, once he has decided, will not waver. And so Maya's wedding may now be in danger regardless... and either way, so is mine. I wish I were sure that Papa would protect my future from Maya's waywardness. So when I see Maya open her mouth to respond, I cut her off again. "Goodness, Papa, what a drama. However could she get married now, when she must return to Chandrapur *to finish college*?"

Papa takes this as encouragement to look at me again, and I must smile, so I do, and I have never smiled this way before for him, and I hate it. Memories of childhood return: of smiling my way through a lesson with Nargis pulling on my braids, smiling my way through a games period with Mawiyyah tripping my feet. When Ammaji made our betrothal official, at least I had Nash to smile at, after school. And so I smile now, broadly, and Papa's honest relief makes my toes tremble. "Exactly as I told her, Leela. Everyone nowadays is in such a hurry. We complain about you children being so overeager to bring about independence, but we aunties and uncles are the impatient ones."

Thankfully, the vestiges of Maya's earlier gratitude stand me in good stead, and she lets me shape the conversation that follows. "I'm impatient,

165

this year, for my wedding day to come. You've told Mausi how sad we are that she will not attend?" Another frustration for Ammaji: our moved-up wedding will be poorly attended, as no one in Kansara can be expected to travel through such downpours. Maya's journey down will be arduous and slow, made worse by Chachi as her chaperone. The placement must begin when the monsoon break ends, though when the actual rain ends only the gods know.

"Maya," says Papa, not willing, quite, to be sidetracked, as though Maya has not sidetracked her marriage enough on her own, "if Mausi gives you any trouble in Kansara, Koyal will tell her it is all my fault."

I nod, and while I do Maya speaks up. "We'll explain how much of an ogre you are, Papa."

"A rakshasa!"

"Frankenstein's monster!"

"A tsuchigumo!"

"What's a tsuchigumo?" Sonuji asks, collecting the empty plates.

"Nash told us about it," I tell her, but I nod at Maya to explain. While she describes his skull-filled belly, while I smile, I clench my fists under the table. If what will happen—what must happen—is not quite what I expected, I will make sure, nevertheless, that it is fine.

"It's not like you to ask me to keep a secret," Maya says doubtfully.

"I'm not asking you to do anything other than what you've been doing already for weeks!" We have dragged the bench from our front hallway to the terrace door, and sit under the awning, soaking in the rain's warm scent.

"Yes, but… I was mostly keeping it a secret from you, not Papa. And Meenakshi knows: Sapan's seen us together in the back room of Pal's Café. She thinks I'm brave… and once you got over your initial impulse, you see how wonderful it is, right?" Maya takes my hand. "I was worried about your intense conventionality, but you're not so bad anymore, are you?"

"Don't be ridiculous," I say. I'd squeeze her hand, but I'm still a bit on edge. Maya will see reason, of course, and keep her transgressions under wrap until I am safely wed—she just has to blather about

167

first, and my tremors will only subside when she's ready. "I wish you'd have fallen in love with Sagar, really, Maya."

She squeezes, instead. "Yes, but see? You're happy I get to fall in love at all."

She's right. I sigh, and watch the rain gather in a shallow puddle where the terrace has sunk a few centimeters. The rhythm of the drops is that of a heartbeat. "You won't have to keep it quiet for too long." Anyway in the village she'll hardly be thinking of Hassan, hardly sneaking off to see him.

"If we get married before the placement, I won't have to worry about Papa changing his mind."

I raise my left eyebrow at her.

"All right, all right—I just want us to get excited and start planning. So it will have to be relatively secretive: I still want a wedding."

I raise the other eyebrow. "Wait your turn," I admonish, but what I really want to do is take her by the shoulders and throttle her: how has she been filled up with all of this want?

"All right, fine—I'm sworn to secrecy. Anyway, do you think it would make sense to get married just after I return, or wait until I'm done with college?"

My sister's feet have been able to reach the floor from this bench since she turned twelve, but today, she swings them, her face bright.

"Does it matter? No school will hire you. His family will probably throw you both out of their home."

It's not my fault that a shadow dims it. "At first they may want to. But won't children change their mind? And Hassan thinks that, well, the dowry might swing it."

This is, in fact, luck I have created for her. A year ago, Papa asked Nash's father if we should marry me off in the modern way, without one, but when the Chowdhurys balked, I begged Papa to reconsider before news reached Nash. "We'll cross our hearts," I say, swallowing the latter half of the couplet. She may daydream her wedding will unite us, but we both know that as the rains drum down, the riots will come.

By dinnertime, we are happier with our secrets. Maya carries her foolhardy wishes close to her chest, and I, in return, bother neither her nor my father about my own revolutionary hopes. When Nash and Koyal Chachi arrive for dinner — for neither can resist Sonuji's idli, made from a recipe given to her by the cook of my father's business associate in Bangalore — I decide not to tell anyone at all. Curzon has steadfastly ignored our swadeshi, the rakhis we tied to the pupils of Bankipore Boys School last October — me to Anis, Nargis to Sapan — and so my anticipation of a reply is my own foolhardiness. But Asoka, ever the Maurya, made overtures to the enemies of his enemies, and I, too, must aim to conquer.

Nash is careful with Chachi in the room: we sit across from one another, suitably distant, and he makes no move to brush his feet to mine, or reach across the table and run his hands along my jaw. That he can resist is unnerving: I want to leap up and pounce upon him like a lioness, sink my fingers into the ropey muscles of his forearms, lock lips. I smile at him, instead, and think of him on the wedding platform, feeding the fire, waiting for me.

Nash, of course, has no use for secrets. "Leela's had a wonderful thought," he tells Papa and Koyal Chachi, spreading his coconut chutney in that silly way that little boys do, as though it were jam, "that if Papa doesn't allow me to go to London to study law, we might put forward another petition, and ask the Directorate to bring a professor of law here." Then he gives me a look so close to wicked I know he is imagining sharing his coursework with me, but in a rainstorm, pallu soaked, blouse sodden. Or perhaps he's just remembering the blouse. I blush, and it's Maya who kicks me under the table.

"A wise compromise," says Papa.

"So long as you put forth this petition, Nash," says Maya. "They all but laughed at us. What a waste of time."

"Petition?"

"Nevermind, Chachi," says Maya. "What do you think? Shall Nash become Chandrapur's leading barrister?"

Chachi doesn't use chutney at all, just drowns her idli in sambar. I don't know why they come here to dine if neither of them knows how to enjoy idli properly. Chachi stops just short of licking her finger after a large bite and says, "A barrister, certainly. Though I support your quest, Avinash, to leave this backwater."

RASHI ROHATGI

We all stare at her, even Papa. Finally, Nash says, "Have you traveled to London, Auntie?"

She shakes her head. "I don't even accompany Vikram to Calcutta, after what happened to—after what happened. Home is fine for me. But for ladies it's different, Avinash; we are at home anywhere in the world. Home is where the husband is, no, Leela?"

She says this as if uttering a kindness. Perhaps, to her, it is a kindness: freeing me of Nash's family, catapulting me firmly away from joint family life. When my Dhadha and Dhadhi were alive, they lived with Vikram Chacha, or rather, Chacha lived with them. As soon as Dhadhi passed, Koyal Chachi ordered Chacha to sell their section of the compound. Chacha didn't have any hesitation about moving closer to us and to the business, but for a while, Maya and I would whine about not seeing Papa's cousins' children, not being able to run with them in the grassy courtyard to chase fireflies. Sometimes we'd beg Papa to claim it back, to give us a proper home, but it came to nothing. But lacking a family home didn't mean I was homeless. The Ganga was

172

my front door, the High Court my boundary walls; I belonged to those who lived within.

"I think you're right, Chachi," says Maya. Grown treacherous with love, has she? I kick her right back.

"Of course I'm right," she says. I concentrate on my idli.

"Almost right, Auntie," says Nash, and I look up, for he has reached across the table and taken my arm. As I feel the ridge of his fingertips against my wrist, I half expect Koyal Chachi to slap us apart, and perhaps it shows, because Nash slides his fingers up the lines of my palm—the lines that have always told of our future together—and hooks his fingers into mine. "Home is where Leela is, always."

My father invites Nash to stay for a drink after dinner. He nods amiably, but his eyes—and his fingers—are still fixed on mine, and as my father makes a louder-than-is-necessary show of unstopping the decanter and clinking the glasses, I feel my shoulders tremble, my knees give way. How could Nash even imagine us living alone together? How would we breathe?

"I'll have mine with ice," Maya says, and Nash's swallowed guffaw brings me home.

"I'll go get some," I say, and we finally let our fingers fall, and as I turn towards the kitchen I hear Nash tell my father about how large the craze for whiskey and spirits has become in Japan, and how he is certain there will be Japanese variants before long, better than their Western counterparts. I've no trouble believing him on that score, as there can certainly be nothing viler than whiskey in its current, fiery incarnation.

I'll return with ice, but I've come to the kitchen foremost to speak to Chachi. She's rolled up her sleeves to help Sonuji with the washing up, but when she sees me she takes a step away from the faucet and smiles. "My lucky girl."

I use the impossibility of a response to such a statement as an excuse to make my request without preamble. "Koyal Chachi, do you think Vikram Chacha would take on Nash as a part-time employee? Of course Nash would be busy with his correspondence course, but I think perhaps it would give his parents some peace-of-mind." I must tie them more tightly to me now.

Koyal Chachi frowns: a bad sign. "He has no business training, beti."

"He could begin for a trainee's pay! He's so quick to learn, you can see." Though of course Nash hasn't engineered anything yet, so I suppose his brilliance is not entirely obvious. I lower my voice. "Papa hadn't any, either."

She tilts her head. "You're not wrong, of course. But he was willing. Is Nash?"

Home is where I am, he said, I want to remind her. Instead, I turn to the icebox, fill a small bowl that immediately begins to chill my fingers. As I leave the kitchen, I see that Chachi is at my back.

"Let's ask," she suggests, more gently than is her wont.

It takes no time to reach the living room, but for a few moments, we hang back, unwilling to jump into their argument about the upcoming meeting of the Indian National Congress. I agree with Nash and Maya that a series of Ganapati festivals isn't going to change British minds about anything, that we need more—homespun and maybe even boycotts—but it hardly calls for their admonishing tone. Papa is no Tilak-acolyte. "And we must outreach further to the Muslims." Nash's conclusion is far more passionate than is required, and I wish he would spend at least half of his day far away from that coffee shop crowd.

"We must," Maya echoes, and I give her a look. Enough outreach to Muslims from her side.

"Oh, come now," I say, taking the seat between Papa and Nash and adjusting my sari border neatly in front of me, "we have Jinnah. You'll look just like him in your wedding suit, Nash."

"Speaking of whom," Koyal Chachi begins, and I am impressed as well as relieved. "Jinnah worked in trade before he trained as a lawyer. Avinash, might you be interested in doing something similar? I'm sure Vikram could institute a traineeship for you."

There is a pause, during which time I bite my lips as Nash takes another sip of whiskey, longer really than one can sip whiskey, I think. "I thought you advised us to go to London, Auntie," he says, finally.

"Well, yes," she says.

"But Koyal is a first-rate planner," says Papa, "and this would be a wonderful opportunity, should you stay."

I am staring at my pattern-less sari pleats, but when Nash says, "Leela?" I cannot avoid looking at him. Our eyes meet only for a moment, for whatever he sees therein leads Nash to look away, and I am left counting his eyelashes, making my wishes.

"Best not decided drunk," Maya says, and Papa takes her cup and pours its contents into his own.

"Excuse me," Nash says, rising, and I rise with him before I think through the matter, but now that I am standing I follow him to the door. "It's been a wonderful evening, as always; thank you."

"I'll walk you to the gate," I tell his shoulder, for he's not turned back to look at me while slipping on his shoes.

"It's raining," he says.

"I've got spare clothes here, all of my clothes," I remind him, but I stand next to him, under his umbrella, so close I can feel his chest rise and fall. "Nash, it's just an offer."

"It would make you happy," he says, "if I accepted." And it's not a question, but I nod. "Leela, please try to understand."

"I'm trying," I say, but I don't. "As I understand it, this would let you study law, let you please your

177

father, let my father leave a family legacy. As I understand it, it pleases everyone."

"All those letters," says Nash, and I can't look at him, so I look out into the night, just as dark as his voice. "Leela, if you've ever once understood me, please understand me now: don't ask this of me."

The Chowdhurys have given Nash everything, and I wonder if he knows—if he understands—how much of who he is now is from Ammaji, from Pitaji, and not just from Japan. He is acting madly. Yet, standing this close to him, what else can I say? "I'm not," I tell him. "I won't."

The gate is in front of us, and Nash reaches his arm out to unlatch it, but then he swings to me, his arm wet on my back, his eyes already closed, his lips already parted. He pulls me in, and up, and as we melt together, I wonder, for a second, if he understands how much he is asking of me.

Zainab's letter arrives the next morning, but it is afternoon before it has dried enough for me to slide it from its envelope and spread it across my pillow. Maya is in the living room, head in a book. Or has she used my distraction to sneak out to meet Hassan against the terms of our truce? I hide the letter with my sheet and tip-toe to spy on her, as I should have been doing all along, but no: today she really is reading, though in the flickering candlelight doing its best to counter the sheets of rain, it hits me with force that she has become a stranger to me.

After assurances that she will implore Hassan to desist, Zainab's letter takes an unexpected turn. *But,* she writes, *must we for each ecstatic moment really an anguish pay? I confess that I had seen him changed, these past few weeks, but thought his high spirits to do with the new school year, the potential for a photographic element to the revolution, to, perhaps too simply, as yet un-despairing youth. He is my younger brother, Leela, and as Maya is yours, perhaps you understand that I am loathe to see his hopes undone. The situation is impossible, of course, but... if I were to marry into a family of some wealth, and you were to follow your intended to London, would it be wholly unthinkable that a marriage could indeed take place? Mere theoretical foundations would shatter, and my brother's heart is a living, beating thing, more dear to me than honor. If the nikah were done discretely, and soon, to be presented to our families as a fait accompli…*

My body is unsure of whether to roil; my mind itself does not know where to settle. First, safest: what does a discrete nikah entail? Though I am sure Maya has taken comfort in the almost-entirely-absurd fantasy of the legitimacy of a mere-candle union, a proper Hindu wedding demands guests, relatives, offerings, gifts. It's infuriating but easy to let Maya dream of what is so far beyond her reach. But Zainab speaks as though… well, it is my sister who must consider the demands of Hassan's faith, not I, and I will leave her to it.

But an entire letter precedes this. Intentionally or not, Zainab has called me back to Mr. Malik's classroom. His enthusiasm for the young Emily Dickenson and what she should mean to us, as young women, as potential poets—here I sighed and carried on with the henna patterns that adorned the pages I should have been using for notes—meant we were all aware that "she was not so far away, girls – just think! Her sister was named Lavinia. She writes not of alienating wandering but of what it means to be, and to think while, at home." We chanted her verse like soldiers that term, Maya and the others aloud, with broad gestures to signify languishing and lament, and I in my quiet corner, not ready, even if I'd been able to speak without being countered, to suggest that perhaps the life of a wife *was* honorable. That even the smallest houses could seem so cold and vast without them.

And it seems that Zainab again molds honor to suit her needs: something negligible. I want Maya's happiness; for what it is worth, I want Hassan's happiness, too—am I not wearing white for his sake as well as my own? For his honor, as an inhabitant of a city that could stand free of Bengal if it wanted, but chose the glue of modern bonds, that chose an independence that Dickenson enjoyed no matter how much she wrote of her life as one of purdah, one of pause. For the honor I carry, I make manifest: a daughter of this soil, with its dreams and traditions. I want Maya's happiness and I want honor, each in equal measure.

Zainab's solution calls for her to get married, as is her right and joy, but why must everyone else's honor call, suddenly, for me to disappear?

Chapter Eight

When Papa comes in from work the next day, he banishes us to our bedroom so he can shed not only his shoes, but his soggy clothes as well. When we return, he is cozy in his armchair in his Jermyn Street robe, reading the newspaper. I've always loved him in that robe, but I realize, suddenly, that he's never been to London. He's had the robe for years, but not since time immemorial—not since before Mumma's death. Did that woman get it for him? If I am banished, will I continue to dress like a ghost, or a Christian bride, in the London smog?

Maya and I squish together on the loveseat; there's a chill in the wet air, and though I'm alternatingly furious with and excited for her, when I soak in the warmth of her toes and lend her my elbow as an armrest, I can pretend this is a monsoon like any other. After a glance at what she is reading, I tilt further towards her.

"Are those photographs of Japan?"

It's a selections of pages from an American magazine, and Maya pushes the pages she's already looked at over to me. The images are hard to look at: portraits, but by technical necessity, they capture but a few moments in time, rather than depicting their subject holistically. Yet, as I look into the eyes of men and women whom Nash may have seen on the promenades, perhaps, or the shops, or in his classes—sometimes I feel a bit closer to the essence of the face frozen there.

"These are by a woman photographer," Maya tells me. She worries her head underneath my jawbone; it tickles. She whispers, "Zaida Ben-Yusuf: Muslim, right?"

"In America?" I didn't know there were Muslims there. We scan the text to see if there are clues as to the photographer's backstory, but the captions only tell us about what is being seen, not who is doing the seeing.

"When I get married," she begins, and then, sensing me stiffen, she drops her voice to a whisper.

"When I get married, you'll come and see me, right, Leela? You won't let Nash's family stop you from coming to the river?" When I fail to nod or reassure her right away, she carries on, as though its only persuasion I need. "They've stopped you from going to school, but that was Nash's fault. You won't need to sneak about anymore to see him: you can sneak about to see me."

I pull myself from our entanglement, and Papa looks up. "Oh, Leela, you've received a letter. Quite a nice-looking one."

I go to the sideboard to get it immediately, leaving Maya with her questions. It's not Japanese stationary; I don't need to waft in its scent (typical, sandlewood) to know that. It's thick enough that its contents can be immediately consumed. It's from the viceroy.

"Well?" says Maya.

Lord Curzon has read my letter! He has heard my request, and he finds it worth discussing further—in person! He'd planned to stop in Chandrapur on his way back to Calcutta this Friday anyway, to drop in at the Khudabaksh library, and hopes that after a public speech addressing West Bengal's recent unrest, I—and any other signatories to the petition I may invite—would like to meet with him.

"Does he want to come over for dinner, or is it a love letter?"

"Stop probing!" I slip the letter back into its envelope, and the envelope into my drawstring-tightened waist. I should tell her, of course; we'll need to write to the others, form a plan to gather before the meeting, to strategize.

"Maya," my father says, but his voice is too mild to serve as a chiding.

"Papa, I think I'll become a photographer," she says, as to remind me how tightly she holds my future in her hands.

"That would be wonderful," he says. "Leela, perhaps if I purchase a camera, Maya can photograph your wedding. We'd all enjoy that."

"Nash's father has already commissioned a portrait," I remind him.

"Yes, but these images would be for me," he says.

"What, so you remember my face after I'm gone to London?" I leave them to their cozy evening. Upstairs, I don't bother with a candle; I just run

185

my fingers over the thick letter and think about meeting the viceroy face to face.

Our letters come and go with no input from our siblings: I tell Zainab of Maya's promise to wait until after my wedding and her placement to resume her liaison; Zainab insists that then the slim window of days between the engagement and the wedding is the best chance we have to marry them in secret, so that during Maya's absence she and Hassan can placate his family. We discuss the third option—somehow convincing Maya to marry, as requested, whilst on placement in Kansara—but such talk fizzles, lost behind a line we've crossed too long ago. Neither of us mentions Zainab's request for me to leave.

I tell her about Lord Curzon's response; his visit has been announced, now, and though Chandrapur's citizens pride ourselves on knowing we will not like what he has to say, most everyone seems to be planning to rustle up their umbrellas and show up at the maidan to listen and then protest. She will pass on news of our invitation to her classmates, and I must tell Maya to speak to ours; Hassan and

Maya may find exhilaration in shadowy corners and whispered words of admiration, but for us, it is in this chance to speak loudly, and state our case.

I take the chance to practice that night at dinner. "Papa, Maya and I petitioned the Directorate to desegregate our college." He pauses, nods, and continues to eat his kitchdi; I glance at Maya and realize she must have told him long ago. Well, she hasn't told him this: "They belittled us and even after we asked others—young men—to put it forward on our behalf, they refused us. But I have written to Lord Curzon, and he has agreed to hear our case after his upcoming speech."

Indeed, he reaches for a paper napkin and wipes his hands, and I must poke Maya to have her close her mouth. "Well done," Papa says, and my smile, tonight, is genuine.

"Could you write to Sheetal and the others, Maya, and ask them if they'd like to join us in our meeting?" I put some papadum on my tongue as she nods, and crunch. "I know he is our opponent, but I think this may be worthwhile."

Papa smiles, and Maya is quick to sense the possibilities. "Papa, could Leela and I go and celebrate at Pal's Café tomorrow? I doubt we'll be alone—Nash often studies there."

"The roads are terrible in this weather," he says, which means 'yes,' of course.

As we are already setting out in the rain, I make Maya let us stop at the Chowdhurys'. Nash isn't there, as expected, but Maya and I sit on the settee, listening to Seema Chachi play the harmonium. If I could make music like that, I wonder if I'd ever feel alone—but my fingers refuse to follow such commands, and my voice squawks and skips out of my control. When the doorbell is rung, Ammaji emerges from the bedroom; I see it's the dhobi, and rush past her to collect the clean washing while Maya pulls open a book.

"Thank you, beti," she says. "Come, help me put this away."

We start with the sheets; in the dim hallway, as Ammaji takes them from me one by one to arrange as she wishes on the high shelves, I wonder which of the sheets Nash has slept on; I wonder if I am holding a pair of his undergarments right now.

I've come craving something plain, and found something salty; I suppress a laugh.

Ammaji places the last of the sheets above our heads; she takes the rest of the pile of carefully folded garments from my arms and leads us into the nearest bedroom. It's Anjali Chachi's and Hitendra Chacha's, but Chacha is at work, of course, and Chachi, I think, in the kitchen—I smell sugared milk being boiled. Ammaji pulls pieces out, somehow, of the monochromatic mass, leaving them at the foot of the bed.

Then she turns to me. "Anamika says Maya is refusing to marry Sagar."

For a moment, the world turns as white as the pile of laundry, but then I realize she must be talking about Papa's refusal. "Maya didn't say anything; Papa was adamant. Mausi wants her to marry Sagar now, at the end of the placement, before she is awarded her degree."

"If only your father would agree to have Maya skip this placement, they could marry this weekend," says Ammaji; as Ammaji's first cousin, Mausi's family can vouch for both sides. Sagar's younger sister can steal Nash's shoes, and his younger brother

189

hide them. "A double wedding is a large expense saved. Talk to Maya, please."

"I think... Papa would prefer the expense," I say carefully. I have been plotting and planning so for Maya to enjoy her West End romance, I haven't given enough thought to how upset Ammaji will really be when she brings shame upon me, upon us. Ammaji will think—she will know—how disappointing I have been, all along.

Perhaps I will get pregnant immediately, so Ammaji's thoughts are elsewhere. Maya will have to understand. Nash will be too busy, then, to remember how we'd once had a chance to be alone together.

"Leela beti, we were content enough to send Nash away for university while you finished school, but Sagar cannot be sent to Japan." Sagar is needed in Kansara, I know, and it is not good for him to wait so long, but—anyway, how does it matter? I remind myself that, college or not, their marriage will never come to pass. It is my own married life I must attend to, so I nod meekly. Ammaji squeezes my shoulder and smiles at me. "I'm glad you're coming to us."

Years later, I will revisit those words in my mind—no, not the words themselves, but the way they strike me in that moment. They are neutrally spoken, fraught with possibility: I'm glad, while others are not; I'm glad you're coming, and not Maya; I'm glad you're coming to us, an entire family, an entity whole and ready to envelope you. I'm glad you're coming to us, and not wasting your time on college. I'm glad you're coming to us, I hear, and not wasting time that is rightfully ours.

"Me, too," I should say, and I plan to say it, plan to pick up the undelivered, pristine pile of homespun and continue to make my way through the home that will soon be mine. But instead, I think of Lord Curzon. He must have come to India for the first time, once, disembarked in Calcutta, marveled at our clean air, and felt himself a child again, reborn while escaping death, at the start of something waiting for him to decide what he wanted to do with his time. In a few days, he may decide he wants to enact my proposal, and then Maya may never have to leave the city at all to become the teacher she's always wanted to be, or the photographer she might rather be, now. It's up to him.

Henceforth, I will kill very few animals, Asoka decided, and it was written in stone, and soon, rightfully, it was so.

"I must check on Maya," I say, and spin, and flee.

In the carriage, I plead motion sickness—and perhaps I would be suffering with the gummy resistance the rains put up against the wheels if my head were not fit to burst already. In the inky wet, the town is changed. On Boring Road, the dinky aquarium walls keep the fish dry; under the awning of the Sacred Heart church, Hindus and Muslims take a few minutes of shelter for a deep breath, a cigarette. We are armed with umbrellas, as Maya explains we wish to be seen leaving the carriage at Tricel, from where we can make our way through the back streets. "We can look at books for a few minutes, if you insist," she allows, but what she means is that she insists, and then uses the money I'd brought for our tea on biographies of Frances Benjamin Johnston and Julia Margaret Cameron. I prefer the latter, and tell her so, but she rolls her eyes at me. "Of course."

"If you're not keen, why did you buy it?"

"Why did you write a letter to—" and she lowers her voice, as if confessing to stealing the zebra from the zoological park, "Lord Curzon?"

But when we get to the café, Nash is, indeed, there. His engineering books sit on a quiet table in the corner, but he is sitting backwards on a chair around a crowded table of jocular young men. His back is to us, so Yogesh Agarwal sees us first, and jumps up to greet us. "Maya! You've brought Leela. Wonderful! Let me get you something warm. Chai? Coffee?"

Coffee? I hang back, and wait for Nash to turn, and smile, and escort me to the table where his books sit, and ask the waiter for chai and cashew marzipan. I should call Maya back, but we are deep inside the café, where no passerby could see us, and I haven't the energy. She has clearly done this many times before.

In this youthful cave, Nash doesn't hesitate: he takes both my hands in his, massaging each finger until it is as warm as his own. Our knees meet under the table, and, free to stare, I am reminded how beautiful he is, but how strained. He is relaxed

193

now – staring at me, I realize, and blush, but do not stop him – but the lines that have appeared in the last few weeks by his eyes match the circles underneath them. "Lord Curzon is coming two days before our marriage," I say, easing in.

He frowns. "Don't worry about that, Leela. There's no need for you to sit on the maidan and listen to his insults."

"Well… there is," I say, and tell him about my letter, and the response, and the meeting. His eyes grow larger, his mouth wider, and by the time I have finished he has pulled me up and into a hug. Dishes clatter below us. "Nash! The chai!"

Nothing has overflowed; we've come out all right. As my cheeks burn, for they have all seen us hugging, now, Nash sings my praises. I hadn't planned on telling anyone else but my classmates, but the boys sense some victory, and quiz Maya, and soon the small back room is abuzz. Not everyone is happy, but I knew this would be the case, and no one confronts me directly about 'communing with the enemy.' Others seem more nervous than is strictly necessary about a meeting that will hardly concern them, unless we are persuasive. They are loud, and argumentative, and I let their voices fill up the room and then say, "Nash, there's something else I'd like to tell you."

But before I can continue, someone else walks into the room. Or perhaps he arrived some moments ago, and I didn't notice, until the flash. As I blink, Hassan pulls up a chair. I should have known. I wonder if I'm supposed to be nicer to him now, or meaner, and settle on neither. "Won't that photograph just be a blur?" I ask. "We were all moving."

His smile is one of relief, and his low growl full of gratitude. He turns his head away from me, and I think for a moment that he's bowing, but when I follow his gaze I see he's looking at my sister, really looking. "She was still."

She turns, then, the way one does when they're being discussed, somehow, and comes to join us. I know I need to say what I've started to say before we begin to speak of anything else, though my fingers have begun to tremble of their own accord. "Zainab and I have been writing to one another," I say, and because my tone is one of a proclamation, Maya whispers to Nash—"his sister"—as though we were in class, and I the teacher. It's easier to say it, I see, if I think of myself like that. "And I was going to write to her to say this, but I can tell you here. When Nash and I go to London as soon as we are married, the fallout of your—" I falter, but it doesn't matter. "The fallout can be minimized. If the Abbasis won't accept you, Papa will. I think."

"He will," says Maya, but it is a prayer, rather than a declaration.

"When you and I…?"

I hear Hassan, then, thanking me, but it's Nash I turn to, Nash to whom I respond. "When. Nash, let's go to London."

This time he swoops me sideways, past the table and its clanging steel and in the small space, amidst the revolutionaries, he picks me up, spins me around, and kisses me. I kiss back because I love him; I kiss back because otherwise, I fear the dizziness that has taken hold will never leave me.

Chapter Nine

"Shall we leave immediately?" Nash suggests. How he can ignore the room's eyes, I don't know: though his hands cup my chin and draw me close, I see Maya's hand in front of her open mouth, I see the boys all agog, I see that Hassan has a dimple in his left cheek. "After the wedding, I mean. Leela, let's." I should have thought the joy would outweigh the strain in his eyes, but with my feet back on the floor, I know something immediately that I cannot explain: all that I've done is not enough.

I draw in my breath, and it sits in my stomach like a stone. I've kissed a boy who wants more from me than kisses, loved a boy who wants more from me than love: who wants more than me. "No."

Instead of tilting his head, he tips the fingers of his left hand and tilts mine. "Well, of course, you'd want us to wait until the roads clear; goodness knows how you've even gotten here today, my water sprite. We are fools, all of us, but—"

I twist my head free, but he blinks, and so I clasp his hands in mine before the moisture in the air can hit them. "We can depart after I accompany Maya to Kansara."

I feel his fingers move beneath mine, and squeeze him harder, and feel my lips pressing down, too, though his lips are not between them any longer. I have lowered my voice so that the others can recover from our kiss, but when Nash responds, his voice rises above their scandalized whispers. "Leela, don't be absurd."

"Nash!" I glare at Maya without moving my face, and she busies herself with her cup and her suitor.

"Nash," I say, with a softness Maya would be unable to achieve even if that had been her aim just now, "you know that Mausi wants Maya to marry in Kansara. You know that Koyal Chachi may not be able to persuade her otherwise. I must," I conclude, because he must understand that if Maya does not marry Hassan upon her return, I will have no way to fix things. I will have thrown away my life, for… sourness is rising in my throat.

He shakes his head, but pauses before he speaks, attempts to match the calm in his voice to mine. "Leela, I know you feel protective of Maya, but she is not easily intimidated. Whereas Ammaji and Pitaji: they are. They will be horribly hurt if you insist on a pleasure trip directly after marriage. At least in London you will be shielded from their ire."

I force myself to swallow, breathe. Does the protective coating of a kiss always fade so fast as this? "You mean that you will be. Nash, if you insist, they will cede."

"They won't!" he says, and though Ammaji and Pitaji are steady in their beliefs, I do not think their fury warrants this. "They won't, Leela," Nash repeats, and I wish we were outside, I wish we were splashed and sodden if only we could also be out of earshot. "Leela, I cannot stay here in Chandrapur without you."

"You can," I whisper.

He doesn't mirror me, but stands up, wrenching his hands from mine, towering over the table. "I won't. Leela, we are to be married. The trip is not appropriate." He sounds like my father trying to be stern, but even less effective, his voice swinging wildly, like a kite. For my part, I feel like a kite-runner who's lost control of the string.

I just have to reel him in, I tell myself, but of course my self is ready with the natural response: Nash? Reel in Nash? The Nash you love would never require reeling in. That is why I must do it, I say, and admonish myself for giving insanity an inch, and stand up, too. The moment I do it, I realize I should have remained seated, should have apologized and tried a different tack, sent Maya to plead on my behalf, sobbing. But I'm up now, and I've opened my mouth, and it's too late. "Appropriate? You've crossed the black waters, Nash, and we're sitting here planning on crossing them again, and you're asking me to be more appropriate? Has Japan made you into someone who'll seek to control me as the British do?"

"Leela," a voice murmurs, but it is not Nash. It is Maya, letting me know that the hand just settled on my back is hers, trying to push me out of here.

It is not Nash; Nash's hands are thrown up in the air, and as he screams I realize I have never heard him scream, not at me, not at anyone, ever.

"I'm asking you to let me protect you! I'm asking you to understand what it is to be a wife!"

For a second I falter. All I know of Nash's arguments with his parents is what he wrote to me about them from Japan. Those were melancholy letters, regretful letters, letters that radiated disappointment, but not hurt. There was no hint of wrath. I trip as Maya succeeds in getting my feet to leave the ground, but not to step away. This sharpness in Nash has been crystallizing since he returned, but I cannot step away from him. "I don't understand," I say, simply.

"No, you don't." Sapan has drawn Nash's hands behind his back, but all it does is make him seem like a panther, about to pounce. His next words are a whisper, for all they change everything. "You understand nothing of being a wife. Maybe you're not ready to be."

And then I really am able to blind myself to everything in the room but his face. "Maybe not," I respond, and then I am ready to go.

I ignore Maya's attempts to talk, Hassan's attempts to shield my hair with his umbrella, until

201

we are in the carriage. "He's not coming home with us," I tell Maya. We are seated, our knees seeking overtures, but I feel as though some strand of me—my heart—has risen above and ahead and is pulling us forward.

She shakes her head, then nods, then gives up. "He'll get off at the maidan roundabout. Listen, Leela, we may want to turn around there ourselves. Go back to the café. Apologize."

After a moment, Hassan breaks the silence. "Not apologize-apologize, Leela Bhabhi. Just, perhaps, recognize that the exchange needn't have been so heated."

"Don't call me your sister yet."

"Speaking of which," Maya says, but more slowly than she speaks otherwise, and my eyebrows have begun to rise in preparation, "I can take care of myself in Kansara, Leela, I can. I want you there, of course—you've known that for ages—but..."

"Slow down here," I call out to the driver. I don't need to look out of the curtained window; the pounding of the rain is always louder over the open field of the maidan, as if the grass does not soak it in, but resists it. "Hassan, I need a favor."

"Anything, Bh—anything."

"Maya and I will miss the appointment with Lord Curzon; we will be out of town. Please meet with him on our behalf; bring Zainab, too, if she is able."

"I will," he says. "Zainab will appreciate the invitation, but with the prospect of riots, and the rains…"

I nod, and then turn my head away to let them have their farewell, their first, really, since becoming viably affianced. I stare at the dark walls of the carriage box and wonder at what I have done, then draw back the curtain and stare at the wide open space and, as the wind rushes in at the opened door, try to conjure up the feeling of Nash's lips on mine, but, with my heart so far above me, fail.

We have been sitting as far apart from each other as possible in the backseat of a borrowed automobile my father seems too comfortable steering. Occasionally, he whistles a few bars, and then abruptly stops, and covers it up by making increasingly jovial conversation about, as he's decided to refer to it, 'our little jaunt.' Papa has decided that we will drive to the village together so he can assure me that Maya will not be married off, and we will all return to Chandrapur for a wedding that he insists Nash won't have called off.

"I'm glad we seized this opportunity to leave town," Papa says, as the mechanical horses trudge us through the mud so deep I am worried we will have to get out and start pushing. I am already dragging my heart along; it seems convinced it can survive outside of my body, in a lemon-yellow compound, without such vestigial organs as a mouth. I force mouth and eyes and nose to focus on the fields that surround us. We've never left the city during the monsoons before, and they are not their usual beckoning green, filled with colorful women, tiny and dark; today they are vast furrows of desire, soaking in the rain with a satisfaction I once thought I tasted. "I was thinking, girls: no one is expecting us yet, so shall we stop in Gaya? Leela, we could finally visit the Diamond Throne."

He doesn't point out that we are in a hurry to arrive so that we can hurry back, which means, I suppose, he doesn't truly believe my wedding will go forward. Maya says, "You should have just asked Nash to join us, Leela; then you two could have stopped in Gaya for an Asoka-themed honeymoon," and as her voice is just as jovial as our father's, I decide to strike her in the gut with my elbow. If Nash had come, his parents would have come, and with everyone from the city assembled in Kansara, there would have been no stopping a double wedding. And yet, if Nash had just come, if he were to materialize in the seat between us even now, perhaps we could… I don't know. I don't know how it would feel if he were to look at me, except that it would stop me feeling, well, as I do. More like the Buddha than his wise commemorator. What would I give for my hollowed-out shell to simply stop wanting?

"Yes, let's stop," says Papa, talking to the reasonable ghost he must prefer to his daughter. "Though I don't believe, myself, that this Siddhartha was an avatar."

I don't, either, nor do I believe that Jesus was, though there are paintings that suggest otherwise, depicting that skinny man on a pale horse. Jesus's arrival was centuries ago, and things in India have taken a turn for the worse. But Asoka built the

Diamond Throne to commemorate Siddhartha Gautama's ascendance to nirvana, so I have long wished to see it. It lies so close to Kansara, just across the river, that we have never successfully visited, always in a hurry to arrive or slow to leave the languorous compound of our country cousins. I can't decide if I'm speaking to my father or not so I say nothing.

Maya is murmuring; no—reciting to herself as she stares at sheets of rain and the wet expanse. "*I am the daughter of Earth and water…*"

As though she'll ever have to see it, the countryside Shelley was traversing. As though she'll be stuck with daffodils in the spring. Maya, who spent her money on a copy of the *Meghaduta* for me instead of on sweets, that first week after Nash left for Japan. Maya, who'd force me to read the lines aloud to her, and purse her lips to keep from giggling at its native vulgarity. Maya, who would have understood how much it would mean for Nash to have sent a messenger behind our carriage, with just one Sanskrit line: *I live by brooding on you.* Maya, who has left a brooding Hassan behind her.

"You're the daughter of a merchant," I tell her, as Mawiyya has oft done.

But I have never done so before, and for all Lord Curzon's ear may yet be mine, Maya will not be put in her place. She shifts as though she is going to turn to me, but she doesn't. Instead, she faces straight ahead and says to my father, "Stop the automobile."

"It's the next turn," he says.

"Stop the automobile now, please."

"Maya, it's not so easy to stop and start again in this weather." So even though she gets what she wants, it's not instant. (So much for automobiles; horses can stop anywhere, can't they? I've never ridden, but it seems to me that we already have a replacement for the horse: the bicycle. Which surely even Hassan and Zainab's maid could be trained to use, though having never ridden one, I cannot be entirely sure.) By the time we ease to a stop in front of the Buddhist temple complex, I have pretended to ignore Maya's face cycle through the entire range of emotions, from fury to furious glee to the face she presents me now: a patronizing neutrality that matches Papa's. Of course.

207

"Papa, would you go on ahead and give us a minute?" Maya asks, and this time, he is out of the car faster than any horse could aid him.

Let her dictate. "Excuse me," I tell her, fidgeting with the door handle until it clicks. "Honeymoon or no, I'd like to see this." And though the rain whips itself through my hair as angrily as anyone, I sigh in relief. I've left my sister behind.

The Buddhists want this site for themselves. We have squandered the truth when it was given to us, they say, by worshipping the lingam next to the holy ficus. Papa shows his agreement even now by ducking under the holy tree's slim branches, contemplating nirvana, perhaps, or at least eternity, but a circumlocution around the god of destruction seems fitting, properly Asokan, and at least in the temple's central hall it is dry. My feet leave prints on the clean marble—someone has been in this morning to sweep the floor—and I want to think about the Kalinga War, and how it changed us, but all I can think about is whether Nash has truly left me.

As if thoughts of Nash have conjuring powers, a group of Japanese monks join me, murmuring to themselves in Pali. A priest emerges, raises his eyebrows, but I haven't brought anything to offer, and the monks shake their head. They are just here to observe, so I bow my head towards the lingam and close my eyes. I want this place to cool the angst inside of me, that ache of hot youth Arnold insists was not unknown even in the Buddha's own day. He survived it by blowing out his own candle; Asoka survived it by uniting the lands around him and bringing them peace.

The monks disappear, and the priest recedes, and I wonder if Nash is thinking about me, worrying that I have left him. Or have I been mistaking his solicitude for affection, his jagged edges for love-shortened breaths? He could even now be making arrangements for London, or he could be arranging to marry someone else.

"You know what Papa just did?" Maya says, and I don't have to open my eyes to know that the prints her feet have left lie flat and wide beside mine. I exhale. "We were under the throne, and he started quoting Dharmapala to me: *Buddhism is for the thoughtful alone.* So of course I knew you'd be in here."

I do have to open my eyes to give her a particular look.

"Can you imagine, though?" she continues, waving the priest away. We should be offering for her placement's sake, at the very least, letting milk drip from tiny spoons in our hands down the dull black stone. "What nerve he has, renaming himself 'Anagarika.' Homeless. As though women have ever had a home to lose."

"But you'll be staying," I whisper. "I've done all of this so you can stay in Chandrapur."

She seems to think she'll be struck down for expressing gratitude. Instead, she says, "It's not unreasonable to be afraid. London is not so close as Kansara." She pauses to let me protest that I am not afraid, but why? Why should I share anything of myself with her any longer, knowing she'll rip it out and twist it to secure her own future? After the silence, then, she continues. "But, Leela, you can't stay in Chandrapur, either, without apologizing to Nash. You're hardly going to become a teacher."

"I might," I say, but weakly. She's left me no choice but to picture it: cold evenings with Koyal Chachi, Papa out to dinner, books spread out across the table. Convincing myself that a life spent truly understanding Pestalozzi was a life well spent. But I could study law by correspondence.

And ask Anis to petition on my behalf every time I wanted to use my legal education to change anything at all about Chandrapur.

But I could study law in expectation of independence.

And if it never comes?

"Leela, even Nash can't be Nash all the time."

"What's that supposed to mean?" Another group of worshippers comes into the sanctum, proper ones, so we let ourselves out, continue our perambulation. We must walk single file to avoid dampening our hips and shoulders, and Maya steps ahead to be first. The temple is beautiful, far moreso than I'd expected. Flowers are cut into the temple railings at every step, interspersed with roundels depicting the tree itself, or fantastical animals: winged lions, horses with men's torsos, arms in the air. There is also a woman with a horse's head, which is a

Jataka tale I don't know. The entire edifice is sharp, fresh, newly redone. When we drive away, I will crane my neck to see the carved stone narrow its way to nothing.

Before the path opens up before the Diamond Throne, in front of which our father awaits, Maya turns. "Offering you Maner and a mother all at once? Leela, if it's acceptance you want, make sure you know whose."

"Not yours, clearly," I say, because what she says unnerves me, and I cannot respond. She is not being fair; she cannot see that I have always stood between her and the unknown, between the streets of our city and the shadowy mother whose lack she does not feel. And as to Maner… let's hope Maya really does marry Hassan soon, because if she falls pregnant—as I won't—I doubt even the Abbasis will make allowances. I push past her, and there it is: the site of ascendance.

"You always have mine," she says.

Leaves have given way under the constant rainy siege, and my toes curl over the edge of one as I stand between my father and my sister and we contemplate my future.

At least I do; after a moment, my father says, *"That great ocean of idealism, in which—"*

"Oh, Papa, please," says Maya. "If you're so enamored, you might quit your beloved Samaj and join the Buddhists yourself."

"I don't doubt it will have a comeback in this new century. You girls don't remember the World's Conference, but the Buddhists were very impressive."

"Perhaps they will hold another one, in London this time, and Nash and I can attend," I say. I smile at my father, for I will not be spending my life in his house, so who knows how many chances I will yet have to smile thus? "Nash likes Tenshin, too. He's quoted him in several letters. Dharmapala less so, but then he's not Japanese, is he?"

My father shakes his head, and gestures towards the car. "Maya, shall we wait inside? I'd like to sit for a bit before we head onto Kansara."

Maya glances at me, and when I speak, my voice is steady. "Papa, let's go home."

He doesn't hesitate, just grabs my hand and swings me around the puddles as though I am a little girl again. I lean into his warm, strong grip, and swallow. Papa will send the Chowdhurys a letter about something silly, some small detail of the wedding, and Nash will understand.

Maya has reached the car before us; from her dripping hems, it seems she opted for the straightest path. "Papa," she says, "I've always wanted to drive a car."

"What better place to try?" I add, though if the three of us die a fiery death in the middle of the monsoon, I'll be the idiot.

Papa shakes his head, leaves my hands to reach into his pocket for the keys, holds them close within his fingers. "Maya…" But she has already plucked them out, clambered into his seat, tapped on the wheel to usher us in to witness her triumph. Until the outskirts of Jahanabad, where Papa insists we reconfigure, Maya carries us home.

Chapter Ten

The day Lord Curzon is to speak, Maya and I awake within seconds of one another. At first I think her jostling must have woken me, but in fact she is sitting up, but quite still. Her expression is quizzical, but not worried, and I realize that is exactly how I feel, and only then do I turn my attention to why: the rains have stopped.

The monsoon in Chandrapur is like the imperial government: upon its arrival, blustering and forceful, intent on cementing its presence. Now: here quite certainly, so inescapable as to render itself almost invisible, and so to counter this it attempts un-foreseeability. We are on our toes, at any rate, whether reaching upwards in hope or not. At least, it means this: the speech will be well-attended.

Yesterday, we signatories met to decide what to say. Because the viceroy knew my name, even my former tormentors assumed I would be speaking for the group. When I explained the situation, watching Mawiyyah's eyes grow was almost, almost satisfaction enough for the whole affair. But not quite: it's true I felt that as a former student, and a soon-to-be former resident of Chandrapur, a passing on of the torch might be appropriate, but it wasn't true at all that I'd had this in mind all along. Though Mawiyyah would have ditched her strict mother-in-law and all the rest of us for London in a heartbeat—as it was she wasn't allowed to attend the speech, nor the meeting, so she was really just here to torment me, which gave my torment of her a bit of added frisson—this small abdication had only been decided two nights before, by Ammaji.

We'd been invited to celebrate the bestowal, by distance certificate, of Nash's engineering degree, but almost immediately, Papa emptied the room of good cheer by telling us his friend had begun to ask her family in England about possible places to live. Nash—looking irritated and proud in turns—froze; it was clear this was the first anyone in the household had heard about our change of plan.

"Well, you'd best learn to brave the cold and the damp, for I doubt Prithviraj will hold your place," grumbled Nash's father, not quite joking, but trying, at least, to salvage the evening. Nash had the good sense not to describe the snow he'd seen in Japan: they'd gone up to the mountains one winter, and the letter he'd written transported me to a fairy's ice box: *it's rain, but in pearls, rain but instead of eagerly awaiting the chance to spread, to merge its single drop-ness to the whole precipitory universe, the water hugs itself for a second longer, its death inevitable but its struggle just as much so. Oh, Leela, what recompense for the cold!* Instead he stood straight, and nodded, and tried not to look quite so pleased as he was.

Ammaji didn't bother to scold him. Instead she held her tongue until Maya mentioned the wedding: how much fun it would be, something of that nature, to gather the night before for the ladies' musicale. Seema Chachi and Anjali Chachi agreed, and before either of their husbands could make the customary joke about how much fun they'd be having peering through the curtains and watching us dance, Ammaji sniffed. "I suppose," she

217

said, and then she looked straight at me. We hadn't spoken since I'd run out of the house, and I'd slid to the front of my seat, unable to settle until she'd called me 'Leela beti,' but she didn't say my name at all. "It's all a bit anticlimactic, now, isn't it? It's not as though she'll really be my daughter, will it?"

Maya had taken my hand, and tried to rub circles on my palm as we ate custard apples—we, I say, though I didn't eat anything after that; how could I have?—and I'd snatched my hand back. Nash undid his earlier gracefulness by telling his mother about my role in bringing the viceroy to Chandrapur; as his voice grew prouder, her eyes grew narrower. "Stop," I whispered to him, and he'd thought it was from modesty, and chuckled as he acquiesced. Or else he'd understood, and wanted me to feel how tightly he could squeeze. No. We are home, and as soon as Lord Curzon grants our wish, we are to begin the henna ceremonies to bring about our wedding, at last, in earnest. He is my Nash, underneath.

"She'll stop all that." Ammaji didn't pose it as a question, and she didn't turn her gaze from my warm, throbbing face.

That my excitement is somewhat muted, then, is only fair. And certainly I expect Maya not to speak until spoken to for a little while longer, but no sooner do I turn to her in order to give her a look of simmering resentment, when she says, "We should go and see Zainab today. You want to say goodbye, I imagine?"

I want her to rein in her imagination, is what I want, but even as I keep myself from saying so, I realize that she is right. There is so much city to say goodbye to and only so many hours left, but somehow I want to spend one of them with an old enemy. Still—"you want to see Hassan, I imagine?"

"You needn't be so arch," Maya says, undoing and then redoing her plaited hair. "It's not like you—it makes you look strange, and old."

"Thank you," I say as archly as possible, but she's right: it's not my forte.

When we arrive, Hassan opens the door for us, looking terrible—pale, wrinkled, like his white tunic. I let Maya whisk him away to the garden to perform, I'm sure she hopes, some rejuvenating magic powered by foolish love. I join Zainab on the settee and for a few moments, we simply sit and listen to the absence of the rain.

"I'm to be married in November," Zainab tells me. "The family's in Calcutta."

"That was fast." She's not showing signs of a tough night like her brother; instead, she sounds quick, open.

She laughs, then glances out towards the garden and stifles the sound. "Hassan took a photograph of me and my father sent it around. It's a 20th century match!" Still smiling, she hands me a tiny plate carrying just three sweets, and I know they are all for me. "I'll miss Chandrapur, you know."

I know.

"But—Calcutta! Perhaps I'll meet Tagore." She begins to hum: *If no one heeds your call…* and, after a moment, I join her. My voice can't be worse than Hassan's growl, after all. *Let the lightening ignite the light in you…*

"Is he handsome?" I ask, when we've found our way to the song's end.

"I don't know," she says.

"I'm sure he'll be handsome," I tell her.

She shakes her head at me. "Oh, Leela, just let him be solvent."

I find out, that afternoon, where Zainab's mother goes in the afternoons. Loathe to disrupt the lovers, Zainab asks if I'd mind watching her pack, and I stare a bit more than is polite as we make our way down the cool, beautiful hallways. Through a half-opened door, I see what I first think is Hassan's camera. But its elephantine protrusion is, I realize, something else. "You have a gramophone?"

Zainab is already pushing open another door, but she pauses, and then turns. "My mother enjoys music. She's a bit mad about championing it."

"My father loves Dvorak," I reply, still looking at its lurid arabesque of a speaker, wondering if my father will buy one soon, after Maya and I leave, to fill our home's empty spaces. "She can come and visit you and see the opera," I suggest, as Calcutta has their own venue for it. Mawiyyah has been, and told us—willing listeners or no—all about the red velvet seats, Cupids in the molding encircling the domed ceiling. I leave it behind, follow Zainab, my mind ready to move forward.

221

She is still paused, however, shaking her head. "My mother, when she was very young, lived near a girl named Angelina." She continues, telling me a story wherein her mother felt protective of a strange little girl, which I assume relates to the gramophone in some roundabout way, but we've stepped into her bedroom and I am captivated. Of course, she doesn't have to share. Her bed is a four-poster, translucent scarves in pale pistachio and rose draped around it; her bedspread is lemon yellow under a layer of lace with imperfections only there to inform onlookers immediately that she must have made it herself. Her walls are bare; her window is latticed, and through it I can see Maya and Hassan speaking and embracing, and turn away. "So you see, Maya will love her."

I can do no more than blink; I can't think of Ammaji any longer. I won't. To think of Maya swooping in, filling the space left by a clearly-beloved and newly-departed Zainab... I want her happiness, and I am happy she will have it. It's not as though I'd get along with Zainab's mother, who leaves her daughter alone all day to – I force myself to think back through what I've just been told — "Excuse me? She became… did you really say Gauhar Jan? The, um, the —" To finish the sentence would be vulgar.

Zainab opens an armoire filled with color — mild, wintry colors, but colors nonetheless — and starts pulling pieces out. Her traveling case is small, but from the decisive way she pulls out each outfit, I gather she will be taking more than one bag. The trip to Calcutta is hardly travel, compared to where I will go. "Yes, the successful artiste. She lives in Calcutta now, of course, so my mother can still come and visit me to see her."

I blink as though another flip of my eyelids will reverse this revelation. Whether or not Maya would have been happy in the village, she would have at least had the option of remaining pure. Knowing Maya, she'll think dancing for men and singing for men — and on records, for money — is the way of the 20th century. "You should have told me," I spurt.

Zainab is still for just a second before she resumes packing, hardly long enough to process remorse. "It's hardly a secret."

"No, it's just never come up at school! In all of our letters to each other! That your mother is—" I feel sick.

Zainab doesn't finish my sentence. She's cleared a shelf; she closes her traveling case and turns to me. "Let's go back out into the sitting room," she says, and her voice is tight. She sounds like the girl who'd let us in that first day, hoping to get her eyes on our syllabi.

But she isn't. So much has happened since then; so much has changed. "I don't know what to do," I confess. "I used to worry about Nash and geishas, and now this. You should have told me," I repeat, because what else is there to say? "You should have told me you weren't what you seemed."

"We are what we seem," Zainab says, dropping neatly onto the settee.

I can't sit; my limbs feel stiff. "You're not," I try to explain. "Even leaving aside the association with the courtesan... you could consider living more frugally if you're so poor."

"Is that what bothers you?" she asks. "That we love beauty, and we save it where we can?"

"I just think…" I don't hesitate to speak to her any longer, but just now I'm unsure of what to say. I've been so focused on my sister staying in Chandrapur that I've forgotten how far away her destination really is. Art is something Maya wants the opportunity to make, not to be. Right?

"I don't think you do," Zainab says. "Think, that is, about us. Me."

"How can you say that?" My heart, of all things, feels shaken, not quite stable in my ribcage. And yet I should have known, shouldn't I, that her beauty was simply a cover, her kindness simply a mask—this house, with its gramophone. I shouldn't feel fragile; I should feel angry, so I try. "I've come to your house, not once, but habitually! I've come to your house knowing that my hours in the town I love are limited!" I've given you my sister, I don't say; I've considered myself your friend.

"Sit, Leela, if you'd like," Zainab says. When I do, she gets up, and I rise again to follow her, but she's just gotten the maid's attention, and she places sweets on the table, and sits again, and there I am. Foolish.

I take a sweet. She's brought them out for me, hasn't she? It sinks between my teeth, and the resistance it offers is welcome, yearned for, and quashed in short order as the sugar slides down my throat. So it wasn't wholly the tragedy that graced Zainab, but this strange upbringing, too, exposed to women who made their own living attending to men's desires. Helping them. Every mystery about Zainab seems solved, now, and if ever I'd longed to be beautiful enough for a photograph to seal my own marriage, well, I'm cured of that. But Maya... it's these in-between women who end up this way, isn't it? And Maya hasn't even fallen through the cracks of polite society: I've pushed her through. I take another sweet and wish I hadn't. My mouth is too full to call for my sister, to take our leave. I glance out at the garden, and at least they are no longer in each other's arms; they seem to be arguing.

Zainab follows my gaze. "She'll miss you terribly."

I shake my head, swallow. "You say I never think about you, but I do. We both do, don't we? You've decided to remarry, and I, well, I've entrusted you with—"

My voice breaks, but before I can recover Zainab interrupts. "Let's say, for the moment, that Maya and Hassan make their own choices, shall we?"

I never should have come here. I never should have let Nash, let Maya, convince me to do any of this. "Don't act like this at your in-laws' house; it's hardly becoming."

I've had the last word, it seems. We sit in silence, and we wait.

When they burst back into the room, it seems Maya hasn't been able to fix Hassan after all. Instead, she looks a mess herself—not happily disheveled, but as though she has been pulling at her own hair. She comes straight to me and pulls me upright. "Leela, Nash has a bomb!"

My first instinct is to comfort her, so I pull her into a hug, and as I do, I catch Zainab's eye, and as though the last half hour never was, we both stifle a laugh. Maya pulls free from my arms and gives a little shriek. "I'm serious. You know he can build one."

The room seems to be moving very slowly, and when I manage to blink it into submission, I see that I'm seated again, and Hassan is apologetically removing his hand from the small of my back. "It's true, Bhabhi," he says.

Zainab hasn't gotten up, and her voice is steady. "Tell us everything you know."

"Not enough," he says. "Talk has been swirling about the riots in Dacca: whether we need them here, too, or whether we can do better using Gandhi's methods. Maya and I have been arguing for the latter, but Nash… and then, yesterday, when Yogesh said that the chance to protest at the speech tonight made riots unnecessary, Sapan said there would be more than protests. At first we thought he meant that he'd start a fight, but…"

"Sapan is an engineer, too." I find my voice. "Why would you accuse Nash?"

Hassan falls silent, but Maya responds. "It's not an accusation. I asked him to dissuade Sapan, and he—well, he said that at first, when they'd drawn up the plans, he'd been in despair about his future with Prithviraj, and that by the time he'd reconsidered, Sapan had gone ahead and built the bomb. And as Nash is the one leaving town, he says it's only fair he takes on the risk of setting it off."

"But… that'll ruin our meeting," I say.

There is quiet as what I've said echoes; well, it's not the laughter I deserve.

"Perhaps you'd better tell him that," Zainab says. "At least, it's a good place to start."

Maya and I dodge puddles like children as we make our way to the café, but when we get there, Nash is not among the young men at the table. We look at one another, and then run back out, dodging more deftly this time. When we get to the Chowdhurys' compound, I tell Maya to carry on home, but she decides to come in with me, promising to busy herself with the aunts rather than antagonize Ammaji – an option I hadn't even considered. As soon as I let her alight the carriage, I regret it, but of course, since Nash and I aren't allowed to be alone, she's right to come.

"Stop hissing," I tell her, as we are let in.

Surprisingly, Nash's father opens the door. He seems older, and I study him to discern why, and realize he's no longer standing as upright as he had been even just the other night. He smiles at us as he leads us to the sitting room, but it's crooked.

"Leela, Maya, my favorite girls," he says, gesturing for us to be brought tea. "Maya, you will visit us, won't you?" Maya nods, silently, disarmed. "Avinash says you enjoy photography. I'm not so familiar, but perhaps I could subscribe to some magazines." We are both reaching at the samosas that arrive as though we haven't eaten in ages, Maya making a show of chewing. "In fact, I could show you a book on Jairam Das I just purchased – almost as realistic as a camera, I think, his brushstrokes."

"Yes, please," says Maya, getting a hold of herself. "Perhaps while you fetch it, you could also see if Nash is about? He'd love it, too, I'm sure."

We stare at our nails while we wait, trying not to think about Papa, though perhaps Maya is thinking of him with his Anglo-Indian mistress, straight-backed and content. But the alternative is thinking about what I will say to Nash, and when he arrives, preoccupied but pleased to see us, I still haven't quite pieced it together. I pull at his arm and mumble excuses, but Maya's on the job, and she distracts Uncle more thoroughly with dozens of questions.

We're in Nash's room, and as the door closes, I hear a sharp intake of breath—not my own. And then Nash's hands encircle my waist and I am hemmed in between his hot breath and the cool wall. "You've never come in here alone before," he says, and when I look into his eyes, I see that he's not preoccupied any longer.

Yes, the conversation we must have is urgent, but it's not a matter of minutes and seconds… I hear our hearts beat together; I feel the soft skin of his earlobes and see that I have brought my hands up to his face, his neck, his hair. If I stand on my toes, I can initiate a kiss.

I stand on my toes, or perhaps he leans down—either way our tongues are like our heartbeats: battling, maybe, or else working as one. The fingers on his right hand strum the line of my spine as though I am a sitar; his left hand dips to fill itself with the curves of my butt—I gasp; no one has touched me there since I was a child, and so the pressure of his palm, even through rough cotton, feels as possessive as a shell on a tortoise. I hear a low, soft moan, and it is Nash, because of my hands reaching down into the split neck of his tunic, savoring the texture: wire on silk, hair on skin.

Wire. I can't bear to remove myself from his arms, but I do pull my head back, and open my eyes, and look at his, brown as wet earth and heavy-lidded. "A bomb?"

His intake of breath is not one of ecstasy. "I don't know how I got here, Leela."

"You don't have to detonate it," I tell him. "Let Sapan start the riots."

His laughter is short and bitter. "He'd pull the green wire rather than the yellow, and blow himself up. He was glad we were sent home—he never would have passed the course." Nash straightens his back, but leaves his arms around me, where they belong. "But… you think we need riots? You were able to bring Lord Curzon here with a letter—perhaps he'll listen to you."

I breathe now more easily; not having to convince him of anything makes it easier to think, and, from within his arms, it's never been easier to talk to Nash. "I'm not sure," I say. "Asoka was able to make the world safer only after he quelled his enemies; the British may have started in trade, but they've tightened their hold on us through force. If I am able to convince Lord Curzon to bring the schools back together, it will be because he thinks doing so will be harmless." I'm talking myself towards a point, I think, but I have to stop to shudder, and taste salt. "That I'm harmless."

"Oh, Leela," Nash says. "I didn't mean to upset you; I didn't mean to end up here at all. If there must be riots, let Sapan take the fall." I'm in his arms, and I want to be, but what he doesn't say is: Leela, you're not harmless.

I nod. "Forget what you've studied—you're not an engineer. We need you in London, learning to speak for us, for India." Why should he have, though? I'm a motherless, merchant class, disparaged teaching drop-out who's let herself be pushed out of her hometown. I'm not made to harm; everyone knows this: Mawiyyah and Nargis and the British and now even Maya, with her insistence on a love that must rip up everything in its path, know that the truth is that I'm here to be harmed. Hold firmly to the truth, Gandhi says. For Nash that means the law, but I picture myself a law graduate, and all

I see is a girl too educated to ignore how much it hurts to be harmless.

Nash nods, too, and I force myself to return to our exchange, to return to us. I stop sniveling like a child; I smile in as comforting a manner as I can, and Nash smiles, and nods again. "I think I just needed you to remind me who I am." He breaks us apart, and I flinch, but he's only retrieving a bag from underneath his bed. "Forget Sapan. Forget riots. Let's go to London, learn how to fight them in the courts, and win." He takes out what I know to be a bomb, but only because of where we are, and what we've been speaking of: it's a strange mass of wires and cells and it's positively frightening. But it's also… well, we're no longer touching, but my heart is still pounding. It's not only love, I note, that sets us aflame.

"For heaven's sake, don't touch it," I tell him, but I don't know how he could possibly refrain.

"I should disable it," he says, but he listens to me, fingers falling away, relieved. "It's just—Leela, I've been talking myself into this and out of this and into this and out of this, and I don't—I can't bear to think that I might talk myself into it again."

One can be talked into anything, I think—into seeing oneself as harmless, into seeing oneself as superfluous to one's own home.

"Give it to me." My voice is trembling, and it sounds like fear, but—oh, Nash, I think, how you scared me when you'd returned. How much you've kept from me, and how much, I decide, I must keep from you. "Come and disable it tomorrow, just—don't touch it."

He wraps it up again, and gives me the bag. We hug, and we both sense the other stretch for a kiss and stop ourselves. "Thank you for saving me. And tonight? With Lord Curzon? Leela, good luck."

The yellow wire, I think. Yes, luck: I will need it.

Chapter Eleven

Maya looks at the bag, and then at me, and directs the driver in the wrong direction. "Best get rid of it."

"We can't go out into the river now; we'd drown."

"Can't we just throw it from the riverbank?"

"For all the time you spend with that camera, you should know that's not how this works," I say, and it's not a lie if I have no idea whether or not it's true. "Look. Go home, stall Papa, I'll take care of it."

She doesn't bother actually saying no, just carries on sitting beside me. "Are you excited for tomorrow?" she asks.

Less than I was, I don't say.

"I used to dream about your wedding," she carries on. "I couldn't bear to dream of mine, but yours... oh, Leela, you'll look beautiful." We're almost at the river, and the carriage is slowing, and Maya slides open the divider and asks for us to be taken instead to "Patliputra… no, the djinni mosque."

"I'd rather say goodbye to Asoka than the djinns," I say.

"They're in the same direction."

At least her mind's off the bag. "Do you think Nash will go back to how he was?" I ask her.

She takes a long time to respond, so long I think she's forgotten. I follow her gaze out the carriage window, murmur my farewells to the market, to the college and the cursed Directorate, to the temples full of gods I'll never see, anymore, in London. I can describe the British isles inch by inch in poetry and prose and still I can't see them. Nash must have felt that way about Japan once, and now he doesn't, but now he can't see himself. And tomorrow, perhaps, he will realize that he can't see me. In the second letter he wrote to me, he was still wondrous, in raptures about the spirit on the streets, but still, I worried. I'd kept something else secret from Maya, then, I remember—such a small secret, it feels now, but still.

Not for long, anyway. That evening I'd come in from bathing to find her lying in bed on her stomach, reading my new book, pulled from beneath the now-useless Kashmiri shawl Vikram Chacha had gotten for me on his last trip, pink and green paisley, thin as a skin between the base of each finger. "Nash sent this for you?" she asked, as though books could be sent from Japan as cheaply as feathers. Still, I nodded. I didn't wanted to admit to her that I wanted to read about Japan outside of what he told me, if only to see the world he drew for me with eyes of my own, nor, indeed, that I'd failed. Though the author was Japanese, the book was about London, like every other book in the store. "It's strange," she said, not dismissively. "Nash sent there, and this Soseki sent to London. They should have switched, and then both of them could have stayed home."

We step out of the carriage into the late afternoon sun; I toss the edge of my sari over my head earlier than necessary to shield my eyes as we slip off our shoes. It had been a strange book, but I'd bought it, and once I'd told Maya it was from Nash it was too late to take it back to Tricel. *What's bigger than*

Japan, I'd read, *is the inside of your own head.* And I'd felt lonely on his behalf, my poor Nash, dreaming, if the world was fair at all, of me.

Maya bumbles in a mosque every time; she tries to find something to walk around and bow to. She'll have to learn. Three black birds swoop in the air in front of us and I wonder if they are the djinns' familiars. Perhaps they think that we are. "I'm sure he'll go back to being himself now that he's sure he can keep you safe," she says.

I know she is right, and for a second I wonder if I should leave the bag here. Nash knows how to be abroad, and he will teach me. Until we are free, isn't Maya right? Isn't London ours?

"That's all I've ever wanted," I say. "Maya, I'll meet you at the carriage in five minutes."

She assents, finally, and I stare at the whitewashed walls, the green cupolas of what I must soon think of as my girlhood. When I think of my mother, I feel chapped lips nipping at my jaw, hear giggles too quiet for anyone but us to notice, taste the ghee on her fingertips under each bite she fed me. Nothing is clear in the daytime; only when I close my eyes is she with me. When I think of Chandrapur, I can see. And what I see is mine, by right, by rite.

If all I can have of Chandrapur are memories, I tell myself, I will at least leave Chandrapur memories of me. We who are to meet with Lord Curzon after his speech are gathered in a small cordoned-off area to the side of the stage. Maya wondered at the bag, but I told her I'd emptied and repurposed it, that Nash had agreed to give up the bomb if I would instead pass on to the viceroy a lengthy, thick manifesto. "What a good idea!" she responded, jealous, ridiculous. She's just as much a girl as I am, and Lord Curzon would use her manifesto for the disgusting British practice of wiping his bum. I apologize to myself, inwardly, for the vulgarity, but somehow it helps me; I'm not nervous, but I don't want my heart to stop pounding.

Lord Curzon has begun to speak about education and how it means more than certificates, more than exams. The maidan is full, but there is a space of about ten feet between him and the crowd. If I throw it there, I tell myself, no one will be hurt. But of course I have no idea. And of course, if it sparks riots, hurt is inevitable. Lord Curzon will remember what it means to be an imperial administrator: people may listen to you, but really they are listening to make sure you are keeping the army at bay.

Nash, Hassan, and the other boys from the café stand across from us, on the other side of the stage—Lord Curzon never should have let them stand so close, but Hassan impressed them with his camera and they agreed to be patted down, as we girls, on this side, would never have been asked to do. They don't look at us as they chant their anti-Partition slogans, and why should they? We are chanting, too, our arms flapping up and down, but even our loudest voices are no match for their latent unruliness—the way they must be watched to make sure the viceroy is not disturbed.

Once it's in my hand, there will be no chance to hesitate, but there's a chance now, and I can't stop myself. Riots mean destruction: of the djinni mosque, cool and quiet at dusk; of Gol Ghar, round and round until the heavens; of the Khudabaksh library, with its books centuries old; of the college, where just once I felt what it meant to be clever. It felt unexpectedly powerful, like the bomb I'm

241

now clutching inside its bag, yellow wire under my thumb.

Pretending to flap my arms up to shout for self-rule, I pull the wire and let the bomb fly.

I'd planned to feign surprise, but the sheer noise of the explosion makes me jump backwards, and as everyone else is doing the same, we fall on one another in a jumbled heap. Then we are being set up by our husbands, our fathers, our brothers, those who have been standing just outside the cordon, supervising. Sheetal's father pulls at my braid; I shake free and reach for Maya, but she is clambering to stand, dusting off a sari that will never be free of the dust of the maidan, aided by my father's strong hand. Once she is all right, they reach for me, too, and before we push our way towards our carriage we stand for a moment and look at the empty speaking platform and at the maidan, heaving with men shouting and throwing punches at one another.

Kalinga has come for the empire.

My father thinks that Maya has to be pulled into the carriage because she is in shock. He helps me lift her as she strains against us, assuming she is simply heavier than he thinks: it's been awhile since he's had to take our weight. When he leaves us to sit in front, I slide myself in front of the door, and Maya leaps at me, trying to claw past me.

She is not delicate; my fingers don't fully encircle her wrists. When she steps on my foot I reconsider my lack of interest in calisthenics. "Get off of me," I hiss.

"Let me pass," she says, as though I am a troll in the middle of a bridge.

"You goat," I tell her, "we must stay with Papa."

She takes my shoulders and shakes them and I wonder if she can smell it on me, the harsh tang of the spark, but the ash is on both of us. "You stay with him," she says. "I need to be outside."

"This is no time to be thinking about…" I can't say his name, all of a sudden, without shivering: has he found shelter? Or has he not even sought it, behind his lens and dreams of testimony? "Maya, for heaven's sake, you're hurting me." She eases her grip, and I take my arms off her knees, and we stare at one another—though I dare not move from my uncomfortable perch blocking the door. "Is this it? Is this the riots?"

"Did you know Yogesh has been seeing a Sikh girl?" she asks me, instead of answering my question, which is fair. How is she to know any more than I do whether the people of Chandrapur will take their chance?

"No," I say.

"They met by accident," she tells me, "at the bangle stand, the one near the corn seller who uses too much lime juice. He hadn't realized they came in different sizes, asked to use her wrists to estimate his sister's. She wanted new ones for her cousin's wedding. She wanted every color of the rainbow, to offset her clothes."

"Okay," I tell her. If she is talking, she isn't trying to jump out.

"They could hardly meet," she said. "No one is calm like Papa, blind like you. She was only at the café a few times. They decided to meet at the speech; she'd pretend to get lost in the crowd, just for a few minutes. The easiest place to find one another, he figured, was right in front. I forgot to check whether they were there."

"I'm sure they weren't," I tell her. "Lord Curzon would have stopped his speech, said something."

"Like what?" she says. "Can he really tell us apart? Know who is supposed to stand together? Stand apart?"

"Well, she'd have a kara around her wrist," I begin, but she wasn't asking, not really.

"When I first met Hassan, I thought—wow. What a beautiful specimen. As though he were a flower. As he taught me about the camera, I thought— okay, so he's smart. And then he started to ask me questions about the way in which I was responding: why did I care more about the aperture than the shutter speed, when the speed was what would enable you to capture a flickering expression, an ephemeral moment of protest? And I thought, well, it doesn't matter, he's just a beautiful specimen, and I explained about blur, and how much it described the way I was supposed to see the present, how much we're asked to simply think of as moving too fast, changing too aggressively to bother with, how much we're asked to keep things still, and he asked me if I wanted to go shooting with him one day.

"I'm not an imbecile, Leela. I had him meet me at Pal's, that first day, made sure that Nash and Sapan and Yogesh saw him come for me, made sure he understood what it would mean if he took liberties. They'd known him from school; I suppose it was inevitable, and then of course he started bringing Anis around to the café himself, our very own desegregated revolutionary society, and we shot everything together: I wanted to capture speed, and he wanted to capture depth, and so together we're a good team, you see—once you realize you agree on how a machine should work, it's not too ludicrous to think you might agree on how this world should work: what else is it, but a massive, complicated machine? Nash agreed with us, at first, with Gandhi: that maybe images of war can replace real war, for who on earth could look at images of war and risk bringing it about? And as Nash began to despair, began to take the others' haste so seriously, Hassan never did. I asked him why once, and he told me: 'ever since I met you, I haven't been able to let anything blur.' And then I kissed him.

"When we came back to the café no one knew, but everyone could tell. They were ready to destroy him, even—especially—Anis, but, Leela, Nash held them back. He asked if anyone knew of a time, a moment, an instance in which I'd ever changed my mind about anything, and no one could, and they washed their hands of the matter. Nash was in such despair by this time, trying desperately to save the country without making you a widow in the process, but he protected us. But the truth was that they're wrong about me. I had changed my mind about something. Now when I looked at Hassan I didn't see a flower. I saw Krishna, the universe in his mouth, my world wrapped up neatly in his lips."

We've stopped, but we're not yet home. Maya falls silent and we stare at one another, and then Papa yanks open the door so quickly I tumble into his arms, and he tumbles to the ground. In a second, he's followed me in, taken my place to seal us in. I can pretend I saw nothing in that intervening moment—it was so quick—but I cannot ignore the fact that along with dust on my hem, there is also blood, and that Papa is holding his wrist gingerly but covertly. "I'm fine," he says, before we can ask. The carriage starts moving again, but not in the direction I expect.

Chapter Twelve

I've sworn to Maya that Nash wasn't the one behind the bomb, and surprisingly, my father provides eyewitness testimony. "I was looking at him just as the explosion took place," he tells us in the carriage to the Chowdhurys, "thinking of what an upstanding boy he's become." We are staying with them, he says, until the violence dies down because without access to the market, a joint family set-up is the only place we will find plentiful proper provisions. He does not mention his wrist again. Sonuji is riding in front with the driver, where I wish I was sitting, watching what I have wrought.

Surrounded by Nash's family, his distant greeting is appropriate, but I have to steel myself for his bewildered gaze each and every time I meet it across the room. Though Maya escapes, I find myself in a circle of middle-aged women, handed a basket of mending and enough white thread to sew Jesus another shroud. It's delicate work at which I do not excel, but every time I prick myself, accidentally or accidentally-on-purpose, I remember what I've done, and am both sick and triumphant.

The streets outside have become stages for impromptu boxing matches, improvised courtrooms, and just plain looting. I've not seen it clearly, but there is an understanding that Curzon will have to report back on the local mood, and that this may push him to take Indian views into account when speaking of Partition, and when speaking of freedom. But also, there is an understanding that there are people who were so recently alive, and are now dead.

What on earth have I done?

No, absolutely not: I've done what my city needed, my country needed, whether or not they need me, and I won't give such thoughts any purchase.

There is the gentlest knock at the door to the room in which we sit – we connect only to the sitting room, so though there is no chance of it being someone from outside I am relieved it is soft, and thoughtful, and when I turn my head I see it is Papa. He beckons, and I pretend not to be relieved to throw over my mending. "Is Maya done freshening up?" he asks. "I was hoping to speak to both of you together."

My blood freezes. "Maya was never in here."

"Oh, perhaps she's snuck into the kitchen," he says, for he has no idea.

He drifts out into the hallway, and I force myself not to run, simply stride forward, seize him by the elbow, turn him with just enough force that he understands there is catastrophe but doesn't scream. "Papa, I have reason to believe Maya is trying to get across town."

Even with everything—even with her life in danger—I can see by the dimmed light in his eyes when I say it that Papa is most upset with us for keeping it a secret. And by us, I suppose, I mean me. "She'll be back soon," I promise, though my stomach is hard as stone and the words come out in stubborn gulps. "She'll just make sure he's safe, and then she'll come back."

Papa is staring at me. "You'll have to stay here," he says, finally, and then he turns.

There is a commotion by the door—first, the usual protests against anyone leaving, but then louder and more specific. I have sunk to my haunches in the hallway corner, but it seems that even if I stay here, I'm not to be left alone. Uncle—Anjali Chachi's husband—is the first to reach me, perhaps because Nash and his father are physically stopping Papa from crossing the threshold. "Get up," he says, in a voice he doesn't even use for the maids. "We'll need all the details you have on this Muslim."

"Leave her alone," says Nash, but when I look at him, his expression is a mirror of my father's. "I know where he lives. I'll go."

"No!" My voice seems amplified, but I realize that Ammaji is crossing the sitting room floor, speaking the same words at the same moment.

Nash doesn't respond to her, he doesn't look at her; he looks at me. "Stop. I have no choice."

We are all hunched together in the sitting room, not mending or talking politics. I am glad that the hollowness of the room reflects the hollowness that has infected my bones, my breath.

Ammaji speaks first, to Papa. "You two may as well go home," she says. "You know you can't stay here when she gets back."

There is a knock at the door—a real knock, on the real door—and everyone jumps but me, who is hollow. The maid opens it, quickly and then crouching, but it is just Vikram Chacha and Koyal Chachi, looking sheepish and then confused as they are bustled in but hardly welcomed. Seema Chachi tells them about Maya, and then about Nash, in tearful whispers.

"What a pity," says Koyal Chachi, and I'm not quite sure she's heard correctly. "Both weddings cancelled." She looks at me, and I want to say something about how lives are more important than weddings, but I don't. "Don't fret, Leela; your sister brought this upon herself."

"Let her fret," Nash's father mumbles.

"Look," Papa says. "Koyal can seem frivolous, but she's right. Maya's choices are her own. There's no reason Leela and Avinash should have their lives upturned."

"No reason?" says Ammaji. "Everyone will know."

"They're just children," says Vikram Chacha, but Koyal Chachi cuts him off. "We all know, but why should anyone? Rumors fly during riots, and then they die down. Weren't Avinash and Leela leaving town regardless?"

I see that Chachi's words have carried the day when Ammaji looks to Nash's father, and then to Papa. "Maya must go abroad as well—and not with them."

"You won't see her again," he says, and after that, things are arranged quickly—perhaps as quickly as they were the first time around, though I have no memory of those days, and just as well. Nash and I are to be married as soon as he returns, and we are to leave on the first available train to Calcutta, and from there the first boat to London. We'll arrive before Nash's course will start, but perhaps, I'm told, we can use that time to start a family of our own. Maya's name is not mentioned again.

Vikram Chacha, Koyal Chachi, and Papa decide that the distance is short enough, and our well-to-do neighborhood quiet enough, that we will wait out the riots, sans vegetables, in our house. As we fasten our shoes by the door, Nash's father places his hand on my shoulder—I've never felt it before, and I feel transported twenty-five years into the future, when Nash's hand, maybe, will be so rough, so wrinkled. "Your mother would be glad you are going abroad," he whispers in my ear. "She loved your father, she cared for my wife—but she hated this city."

We sit, straight-backed, at the kitchen table; we have been sitting here for two days. Chacha and Chachi left yesterday, after a harried messenger brought us a note from Nash: *Maya is safe, but unwilling to return. I am at home. Riots subsiding, but streets not yet safe. I see that I am beloved no longer.*

Papa slams his fist on the table, and I sigh and get up. I sit beside Papa as he maneuvers the horses through the streets, and I hold my hand to my nose and mouth. There are bodies. There is blood. This is not the memory I have of Mumma, long-limbed and eyes closed, her body laid out on its way to the crematorium. The beautiful buildings recede into the background, a droning veena for the anguished melody of passions ignited, ablaze, and then burnt out.

The maid opens the door to us, first unabashedly poking her head through the window to make sure we are not there to loot. Zainab and Maya are seated on the divan, and for the first time in some years I am face to face with her parents. The bags under their eyes hardly mar the elegant lines of their faces. What does Hassan, surrounded by beauty, see in Maya? And where is he? I look to Maya, but when she catches my eye she looks down, as though finally demure. I look to Zainab, and she tilts her head slightly to the empty space in the living room where the camera otherwise sits.

We are seated; we are brought tea. The Abbasis wait for Papa to speak, and when he does, the lines above their eyebrows melt, and their eyes soften. "I'm sorry I did not anticipate and formally seek a betrothal between my daughter and your son," he says.

"We also apologize."

"I would like to have the nikah at my home," Papa says, and he takes Maya's hand. "Tomorrow, if it suits you."

"And the Hindu ceremony?" Maya asks. Now that I'm not the one seeking her eyes, she lifts them.

Papa shakes his head. "We live in a modern world," he says, "but we live in an ancient city. Your choice to marry into this family means that you must outwardly renounce your faith." He glances at the Abbasis, but continues speaking to Maya. "And, after the wedding, Leela's sasural has asked that it be understood in our community that Maya has gone abroad."

There are nods.

"Will you come back with us tonight, my darling?" Papa asks Maya.

She shakes her head. "It's too late, Papa."

"Maya," I entreat, and when my voice breaks, she looks up, finally, at me. "One night. Please."

We turn to leave; it is best to be off the streets as early as we can manage. At the door, Zainab hands me a letter, and taking it from her hand, though I'm out of practice, I try and smile.

We were right to leave, because when we return home, our gate has been opened and Sonuji stands in front of the door. "Chowdhury sahib," she explains, "Avinash is here, and, well—a visitor."

257

Papa walks through, clutching Maya's hand so tightly I daresay she could not have stopped moving forward if she tried, but I stop in the doorway. In my living room, sipping tea with Nash, is Lord Curzon. He stands up and extends his hand to Maya. "Miss Leela Chowdhury?"

Maya doesn't shake it.

Papa clears his throat. "Viceroy, welcome. May I present my daughters, Maya—" and now she is forced to reciprocate the greeting—"and Leela Chowdhury." I rush forward, then, and shake his hand.

"I'm so sorry I wasn't able to meet with you earlier," he tells me, and we sit. I clutch Zainab's letter like a shield. It doesn't seem that he knows. It doesn't seem that Nash has told him anything. "I was impressed by your commitment to the pursuit of learning. Your fiancé tells me you'll be taking up jurisprudence next, in the capital."

After a moment in which I realize he means London, I nod.

"I'm sorry you'll be leaving such a vibrant city," he says. "The citizens of Chandrapur clearly thirst for education. And I'm sorry, as well, that further talks with the Nawab and the Maharani have made it clear that—well, as recent events show, perhaps segregation is best for everyone right now."

"I—that's not—"

"I was going to invite you to formally become a liaison for the West Bengal Directorate of Education, but at the very least I'd like to thank you for bringing the issue to my attention."

And we haven't even sat, and he's leaving, and I've said nothing of substance—though I suppose I have managed not to confess to the imperial authorities that I've committed treason. But not without reason! And not—as he walks towards the door, I realize that it's not enough: to throw a bomb and then fade away. Nothing will ever be enough, but at least I have my sister. "Segregation is not best for everyone right now," I begin, and he turns back to me. "The riots should indicate to you that we have voices, and we are willing to do all that it takes to make sure they are heard. If we hurt ourselves, it's because we must show you that we bleed as much as any other British subject. But we are one people, and my sister, Maya—we speak as one. If you continue to segregate the schools,

259

she will be forced to leave school, too—let her be your liaison."

I'm not sure I've made sense, but the viceroy is listening, and Maya wastes no time in shaking his hand again, this time with vigor. "Let me switch to the Muslim college," she says. "I'll report to you: I'll show you that we work for peace. When the time is right, we can speak again to the Nawab and the Maharani, and make sure Chandrapur's students are all properly given access to the life of the mind."

"Well," he says. "Well, yes. Why not?"

"Please carry on making arrangements," I say, quietly. "Excuse me."

My father doesn't bother to ask us not to close the door, so Nash and I have peace and quiet, but my betrothed lingers at the room's entrance, unwilling to bridge the distance between us.

"Sit at the vanity," I suggest, opening Papa's armoire.

As I take Papa's traveling chest out of its resting place under his hatboxes and lay it open in front of me, I try to convince myself that speaking to someone you can't see is just like writing them a letter. "I'm sorry I stole your bomb. It seemed like you'd have regretted throwing it, not least because you would have been caught, and arrested."

Next, I take our Mumma's chest; it's older than Papa's, as he must have found the need to spring for something more modern at some point. I wonder if he couldn't bear to look at the matching piece after she died, or if it was simply a matter of practicality. I take out the saris, one by one, and transfer them. I take out the shoes, and then I am crying, and when I return them to Mumma's chest, they are marked with my tears.

"Leela," Nash says, and he's left the chair, and he's wrapping his arms around my back, wiping each tear, uselessly, as it rolls from my cheeks. "You started a riot. People are missing: Yogesh has not been seen since. Leela, you caused people to die."

I nod, because what apology can I provide? Did I advance the cause of justice, or thwart it?

"Come to London with me, and we'll leave this all behind," Nash says.

I close the case, I close the chest, and I agree. When our lips meet, then, I know we have both delayed the questions we will ask ourselves, and ask each other, until we are so far away that no stone in the city could absorb our voices. Until we reach a cold, grey city, quite soon, together.

After the viceroy and Nash leave, Papa pulls us to him on the sofa and we sit, nestled in his arms, until he falls asleep. We return to our bedroom together, but all Maya says to me is, "A bomb, Leela—how could you?"

Faced with silence, I light a candle and read Zainab's letter.

Dear Leela,

When the riots end, and when Bengal is again united and India is free, people will look back on this day. I will see a classmate, a friend, who by the time we are free will live in a city full of people who see her Asiatic attire, so outnumbered, so backwards and worthy of what violent feelings it may engender and who may, perhaps then, know how I feel. Hassan sees someone different: in the photograph I enclose, Maya stands at the center, her voice shouting, her eyes ahead, but you—you throw a small round object high in the air with complete and utter faith in the freedom it will bring. He says he will not share his copy with anyone; and yours is for you

to make public as you wish. The riots were coming, he
says, and he commends your bravery, though he weeps
for those of his friends, those of his classmates, you have
caused to be harmed.

Until the riots end, until Bengal is again united and
India is free—write to me. I will feel safer, not least for
my new sister, knowing you are across the sea.

Zainab

Zainab squeezes my right hand, and Nash my
left, as Maya and Hassan's carriage begins its journey
across town. The salt of my tears gets caught in the
hardening paint that has turned my lips bright red.
I want Maya to turn her head, to smile at me one
last time, but we've agreed.

Zainab squeezes twice as hard for a second, and
then slips her hand from mine. Her family must
depart as well and take the shortcut through the
college grounds to ensure that they are at home to
greet Maya and Hassan when they arrive. Nash's
family—my family—has long gone. They preferred
not to witness the nikah. In a few minutes, Nash
and I will join them for what was supposed to be
the first lunch of the rest of my life but will in fact

have only to symbolize what we are leaving. The Calcutta train leaves at five p.m. sharp, and we will be on it.

Papa picks up the hand that Zainab has left hanging. I turn my head, and his face is surprisingly dry. Perhaps tonight he will cry into his lover's arms. She has been patient. When I write to him, I will imagine her sitting across from him at the table. It may make me angry, but I think it may make me feel happy to know she is there. It will make him happy to know that when we reach London, we will not quite be among strangers. Her aunt and uncle aren't Nash's parents, but they have agreed to have us as paying guests in a city where it's not so easy to find a place. "My daughters," Papa says. I don't know how to respond.

"I'll go and get your things," Nash says, dropping my hand, and I know he is giving me and Papa a chance to say goodbye. But, although we've made no agreement, I can't bear the thought of being in his arms without Maya nearby.

"I'll do it," I tell them.

The door to our childhood bedroom is shut, and I leave it. Instead, I push open Papa's door and sit on the bed. I open the chest and stare at the layers of white cotton. I am leaving so much behind, but this one wooden box is coming with me. Mumma's saris are only across town, but they are already nowhere she would have expected them to go. Her saris, her daughters: dispersed.

I close the chest. For a moment, I am alone.

Acknowledgements:

Thank you to Anand A. Yang, whose *Bazaar India* (UC Press, 1998) showed me my family history in print – and introduced me to the antics of the Edwardian-era Rohatgis. Special thanks to all of the Rohatgis whose traces appear here, especially the inspiring Pauline Rohatgi, whose interest in art Maya shares, and Ram Bihari and Urmila Rohatgi, whose dreams of Japan inspired me to seek out those connections. And of course, thank you to the inimitable Malti and J.N. Rohatgi, without whom this book would not exist.

My gratitude extends towards everyone who's ever read a page, or heard a snippet, of this book during its formation – including but not limited to Rasma Haidri, Faiqa Mansab, and Emily Robbins – and to all the gatherings of writers, both nameable (thank you, AWP!) and un-nameable, who became my community. Thank you to Lauren Haynes and everyone at Galaxy Galloper, who found my story and brought it to life, and to Fauzia Burke. Thanks, also, to Prachi Gupta, Kavita Kharecha, Sarah McGill, Jim Cordes, Snigdha Sah, Rebecca Jones, and Deepshikha Dhamija, for listening.

Thank you to everyone in London, in the Valley, and in Bodø who gave up a seat for the pregnant woman, or smiled at the baby, so I could think about my story for a second. And finally: thank you, Mom, Dad, Bhaiya, Ranjan, Kylee, Jamie, and Jawahar, for everything.

The following lines have been quoted in this novel (with varying degrees of accuracy by the characters). Due diligence has been made to acquire permissions; any further correspondence regarding these can be directed to the author.

Kalidasa. "Look to this Day."

"Meghaduta." trans. C. John Holcome. Ocaso Press, 2008.

Basho. "Along this road…"

Dickenson, Emily. "Compensation."

Byssche Shelley, Percy. "The Cloud." *Prometheus Unbound*.

Dharmapala, Anagarika. *Return to Righteousness*.

Tenshin, Okakura. *Ideals of the East*.

Tagore, Rabindranath. "Ekla Chalo Re."

Soseki, Natsume. *Sanshiro*. trans. Jay Rubin. Center for Japanese Studies, 2002.

CPSIA information can be obtained
at www.ICGtesting.com
Printed in the USA
LVHW020826060820
662299LV00001B/69